12 Ghostly Tales

K. B. Goddard

ISBN-13: 978-1517070861
ISBN-10: 1517070864

A CIP catalogue record for this title is available from the British Library

Cover design by Andy Buckland
Contact: andybuckdawg@hotmail.com

Dedication

To Bernadette for all her support

Contents

The White Lady

'After Breakfast, I shall give you a proper tour of the house and grounds,' Mr Samson was saying to his friend Mr Palmer. 'I think you'll find several of the rooms a good deal more cheerful by daylight.' Palmer had arrived on the previous evening and was at once struck by the rather gloomy and forbidding atmosphere of the house.

'I should like that very much. I have been looking forward to seeing some of the paintings. I understand that your family have quite the collection?'

'Goodness yes; my grandfather was always buying or commissioning some work or other.'

'Do you possess anything by the local artist, Mills? I have seen a couple of his landscapes; they are really very fine works.'

'Why yes, as a matter of fact, I do have one of his paintings. There's a story connected with it which you may care to hear later.'

'I should be delighted.'

When they had finished their breakfasts, Samson walked his friend through the house as they conversed lazily. They stopped here and there to admire one or other of the numerous antiques collected by the Samson family down the years.

Eventually, he led him through a long panelled gallery, the walls of which were hung with various paintings of different periods; amongst them were many family portraits from several generations past.

As they approached the far end of the gallery, Samson paused beside one such portrait.

'I promised you,' said he, 'that I would show you the Mills painting; and here it is, though I'll wager it isn't what you were expecting.'

'No,' exclaimed Palmer, 'I hadn't the least idea that he had produced any portraits. I know him as a landscape artist only.'

'As do most people. I don't believe he did many such paintings, certainly. Well, what do you think of her? She is rather striking do you not think?'

'I do indeed.' It was true; the painting was of a statuesque young woman, dressed in the classical style of the early part of the century. She was tall and slender with a delicate nose and warm, intelligent eyes. The merest hint of a smile touched her pretty pink lips.

'She is quite wonderful; but who is she?'

'She is the youngest child of my great-grandfather.'

'But how came she to have her portrait painted by Mills?'

'Well, it seems he was introduced to my family by some mutual friends. My ancestor, being something of a patron of the arts, was much taken with the young man. He soon became a regular visitor here.'

'But surely there is something in this girl's eye that tells of more than a friendly acquaintance?'

'Ah, you see that do you? Well, you are right, and perhaps it does show. She was at one time engaged to Mills.'

'Engaged!' said Palmer in surprise.

'Yes, as you may possibly know, Mills, though a generally well-regarded artist, was not particularly a wealthy man. He was, however, of noble stock for all that. His family had in recent generations suffered a decline in fortunes, yet there was still a small estate, though little with which to maintain it, and a title to which he would one day succeed. So, it was not altogether unnatural that her father should agree to the match.'

'I see, but surely there was more to this than a business arrangement?'

'Well, she loved him desperately, as young girls will, with all the fierceness of youth. He on the other hand, though apparently fond of her, seems to have felt a far greater attachment to her wealth. Of course, that didn't signify, many a good match has been built on worse foundations. There was just one obstacle to their happiness; it transpired that this young man was already married! It seems that, in one of his less inspired moments, he had rashly committed himself to the daughter of an Innkeeper, somewhere in the north, in whose premises he was staying. Having rapidly repented of his decision he soon abandoned his new wife.'

'Good heavens!'

'This poor girl,' he said indicating the portrait, 'found out on her wedding day of all days, during the service as a matter of fact. The wife somehow got wind of his plans and turned up at the church, babe in arms, raging like a fury, and who could blame her? It was too much to bear. The poor girl was grief-stricken and out of her senses. Anyhow, in the confusion that followed she fled the church. By the time everyone had recovered from the shock and realised that she had gone, she was nowhere to be found. When she did not return to the house the alarm was raised.

'By that time there was an almighty storm brewing, and there were grave concerns for her safety. A search party set out in pursuit, but the storm broke before they could find her. The men searched on, though they could barely see where they were headed through the fierceness of the rain. Eventually, she was found wandering on the hillside opposite. The poor girl was soaked to the skin, shivering and delirious.

'They got her back to the house, put her to bed and kept a fire burning in her room through the night. Apparently, in her more lucid moments, she cursed her treacherous lover. Well, the fever took her in the end. They say Mills was a broken man from that day on. He died within a year when his carriage overturned one evening on a bridge, not far from here, during another storm. Some say it was the lady's revenge.

'It is said that she often walks abroad, on nights such as that, seeking to punish faithless lovers. She is often referred to as the white lady.' He smiled on his guest, pleased with his family legend. 'It is a fine example of the British country house ghost is it not?' His companion did not answer for a moment but instead stood staring at the portrait, one hand fidgeting with his watch chain. Finally, he roused himself.

'It is certainly an intriguing piece of family history, but surely you do not believe such tales of avenging spirits and phantom brides?' he asked. Samson's eyes drifted toward the restless hand.

'Well, maybe I don't and maybe I do, old man; but I don't intend to put her to the test. In any case, I am a confirmed bachelor! So she's not likely to trouble me. Ah, but this is a fine discussion for a man about to marry!'

'Indeed, I can only hope my own marriage is more fortunate.'

'I dare say!' his friend laughed. 'Anyhow, let us not linger here all day; I have still not shown you the grounds.' He pointed out of the nearest window. 'You see over there, just beyond that hill, there is the ugliest folly you are ever likely to see; it must be seen to be believed.' With that, he led his friend away to continue their tour.

***

The following day, while Samson was engaged in business elsewhere, Palmer went for a walk in the grounds. It was a cold day and blustery too. He gazed out across the gardens just as a heavy black cloud obscured the sun. The ordinarily pleasant looking grounds took on a dark, and almost sinister, aspect in the murky half-light. The place seemed to him to be filled with deep, forbidding shadows. He did not care for the house, though he would not risk offending his friend by giving voice to the thought.

He decided to pass some time in taking a turn around the maze, but having found the centre he did not linger; it was not a very cheery spot. As he retraced his steps, he was startled to hear footsteps behind him. He was surprised at this as he had believed himself to be alone. He turned, expecting to see one of the gardeners about their business, but he saw no one. This did not worry him; he merely assumed that the maze had somehow distorted the direction of the sound. He turned back and again began to retrace his steps.

The sound came again. This time he was quite sure the footsteps were directly behind him and closing rapidly. He span around in alarm. This time he saw a flash of white as a figure disappeared into another avenue. His curiosity piqued, he ran after the figure; he saw no one. He ran on, through the maze, searching, but he could find not the slightest trace of its other occupant. By this time he had wandered some way from the correct path and took a good many wrong turns in trying to find his way again. He was relieved when he finally broke free from the confines of the maze; the atmosphere within was dank and oppressive. He inhaled deeply; the air was sweet with the promise of rain.

Shaken by his experience in the maze, and in the expectation of rain, he returned to the house. He decided that he would visit the gallery again and look more closely at one or two of the paintings that had struck him the day before.

When he found himself once more before the portrait of the unfortunate bride, he paused. There was something in that beautiful face that reminded him of his own betrothed. The rain had by this time begun to trickle languidly down the windows. He ran his eyes over the girl's delicate features but was surprised to see that there appeared to be a harshness there, which he had not observed before. The painted eyes before him seemed to stare out of the canvas, watching him.

He found himself feeling suddenly greatly discomforted in the presence of the portrait; he could no longer bear to look upon it. He turned his back on those searching eyes and quitted the room.

✳✳✳

That night, the two men sat in mutual comfort on either side of a blazing fire. The fire was a cheering sight, for the night was a bitter one, and the wind roared around the old house, rattling the windows as it went.

'I am sorry to have left you so much on your own today,' said Samson, 'but I'm afraid I had some business which couldn't wait. I trust you got on all right?'

'Oh yes, yes. I took a turn around your maze and had a good look at some of the paintings you were good enough to show me yesterday.'

'Good, good. Well, I promise to be a more attentive host tomorrow at any rate. Perhaps we shall call upon my neighbour Jenkins. I think you'll like him; he is a most amusing fellow, and he has a remarkable wit. He is always pleased to extend his circle of acquaintance.'

'I should be delighted.' Samson sipped his brandy and sighed contentedly.

'There really is nothing quite like a good fire and pleasant company on a night like this.'

'Indeed,' said Palmer, 'one must pity any poor soul who should chance to be caught out tonight, for it looks like being a monstrous storm before morning.'

'It is a night fit for the white lady to walk,' said Samson in an awe-inspiring tone. He laughed at his jest as he put down his glass and stretched himself. Palmer did not share his mirth. 'Well, I don't know about you, but I'm for my bed.'

'Yes, I think I'll turn in too, though the wind seems likely to keep me awake half the night,' said Palmer, listening to the melancholy moaning of the wind.

Candles in hand, they made their way upstairs. Halfway up a sudden gust of wind blew out Palmer's candle, and he muttered an oath.

'Not getting nervous with all this talk of ghosts are you, Palmer?' asked his friend jokingly. Palmer leaned uncomfortably on the bannister, peering down into the darkness. 'Not to worry, mine hasn't gone out at any rate,' said Samson. 'Let me relight you;' as he did so Palmer remarked,

'I don't suppose you keep a cat do you, Samson?'

'A cat! Goodness me no. Never could stand the wretched creatures. What a strange question; why do you ask?'

'Oh, it's just I thought I felt something brush against me just now when my candle blew out. I must have been deceived by the wind.'

'Yes, just the wind. I'll wager the window in the passage has come open again; I've been meaning to have that looked at.' As they reached the first-floor landing they saw that the offending window was indeed ajar; Samson fastened it, and the two friends took their leave of each other.

Once inside the confines of his own room, Palmer turned the key in the lock; he could not have said why. There was an undoubted chill in the air, despite the fire which had been made up for him; an extravagance to be sure but one he was only too glad of. It was a pleasant room enough, with a comfortable chair and bed, and solid but not unattractive furnishings. It was a room conducive to a good night's rest.

Yes, it was a cheery room; but Palmer did not feel its influence. His mind was on other matters. Placing his candle by the bed, he undressed quickly and slipped beneath the covers. He did not blow out the candle immediately but lay for some time in thought. He reflected on his experience on the staircase. He had told Samson that he had been deceived, but he admitted to himself, now that he was alone, that he did not wholly believe that to be the case. In truth, he was certain that he had felt something, or someone, brush against him. It wasn't a mere gust of wind for there was a very tangible feeling of touch, of motion.

It was fancy, nothing more. He was a rational man. He put the candle out and settled himself to sleep. He had not long since closed his eyes when he felt an irrepressible urge to open them again. He was sure, yes absolutely certain, that someone was watching him and with no very benevolent gaze. Instinctively, his eyes sprang open, and he peered into the gloom. He saw nothing. He was aware, however, of a damp smell in the air. He was sure it hadn't been there when he had first entered the room; still, he would mention it to Samson in the morning. Perhaps the old roof was leaking in the rain.

He closed his eyes again; again the same sensation passed over him. This time, he refused to open his eyes. It was folly to give in to such nonsense. He remained in that attitude for some time until sleep finally overcame him, and he drifted into an uneasy slumber.

In the early hours of the morning, when the promised storm was at its pinnacle, the rain beating in furious waves against his window, he was dragged from sleep; but it was not the storm that had woken him. In his half-wakeful state, he was suddenly aware of a musty, earthy breath against his cheek. To his horror and revulsion, he felt pressed to his lips a cold, clammy kiss.

He recoiled in horror from the touch; springing from the bed he hurried, with shaking hands, to relight the candle. He looked about him feverishly. To his momentary relief, he saw nothing. It is just possible that he may have passed the sensation off as some diabolical nightmare had it not been for the sound which greeted his ears, a soft, low laugh, of such utter malevolence as to stop the blood in his veins.

The laughter came again from behind him. He turned slowly and was confronted by a face, bare inches from his own; a woman's face. He recognised her in an instant as the woman from the portrait; there was no beauty now in that terrible face. Oh, what a face it was! If ever a countenance spoke of absolute hatred and loathing it was hers in that moment. She was dressed as a bride, but not such a bride as any mortal man would wish for. Oh, that hideous vision!

In a heartbeat he was at the door, clambering at the lock and flinging himself into the passage beyond, the hideous, mocking laughter ringing in his ears. In another moment he was clawing desperately at his friend's door. The door swung open, and Samson, greatly alarmed, looked on in bewildered horror as Palmer collapsed, insensible, on his threshold.

With the help of the servants, Palmer was conveyed back to his bed, and the doctor was sent for. It was some time before he regained any degree of consciousness; even then his moments of lucidity were brief. Several times he called out,

'Keep her away; for God's sake keep her away.' In those moments he would throw out his hands, as if to push someone from him, with such violence that he had to be restrained to prevent his falling from the bed. This of course was put down to delirium, brought on by fever. It is possible that Samson may have had other suspicions, but if so he remained silent upon the point. The morning wore on and Palmer weakened. His eyes opened briefly once more, and he cried out in distress,

'She sees into my heart. She sees all. She knows; she knows. For pity's sake have mercy!' For days he lay in that condition, delirious and fevered, until he eventually succumbed.

Palmer was mourned by a pretty, kind-hearted, and it should be noted, wealthy fiancée, whom he was to have married a month from the date of his demise. It is likely, however, that she would have mourned him less fervently had she been aware of the contents of certain letters found amongst his papers. These letters, written in the hand of another young woman, showed a side of Palmer's character which was wholly unknown to her.

Why Palmer kept such letters I can only speculate. Perhaps his conscience already reproached him; perhaps, after all, he had intended to make some small effort to relieve his guilt. His parents, a kind-hearted and honourable couple, I believe did all they could discretely do to assist the unfortunate letter writer. When last I heard of them, they had found comfort in the guardianship of a charming little girl, a distant cousin of Mrs Palmer's by all accounts, who was tragically orphaned soon after birth and adopted by the couple.

So, dear reader, let this serve as a warning to those of guilty heart; if you should find yourself in that part of the world, on a night when storms rack the sky, then beware the white lady, for she walks abroad for you.

Three Knocks

The landlord of The Rose and Crown was warming himself on the dying embers of the fire. The snow, which had been falling heavily all day, was still coming down in earnest. His eyes strayed to the clock; the hour was late, and his thoughts were turning towards bed. His wife came through from the kitchen.

'A quiet night tonight, my love,' said he. 'But then it can't be wondered at; 'tis no night to be abroad.'

'Have you barred the door yet, Bill?'

'No, my dear; I was just about to.'

'I wish you would.'

He threw the fire a last wistful look and went about his duty. His wife watched him closely, sighing as the last bolt slid into place.

'There we are, safe and sound for the night.'

'I wonder.' The words were barely more than a whisper, but he caught them. He said nothing but placed a comforting arm around her. She looked up into his worried face, then from him to the door. He extinguished all but one of the lights, leaving the little bar-room in near darkness, a single candle the sole point of murky light in the gloom. Taking up the solitary light, he guided his wife gently to the stairs. He could feel her trembling. She climbed slowly, one unsteady step after another. Halfway up the stairs, they were halted sharply by a sudden, heavy pounding on the door below. The woman cried out, shrinking back against the wall. The banging came again, more insistent than before.

'Oh Bill! There it is again. Whatever can it mean?' The landlord did not reply, instead, he cautiously retraced his steps into the tap-room below. As he reached the front door it came again, three loud and urgent thuds upon the door. The door shook on its hinges, and the sound seemed to fill the little inn. The landlord snatched open the door, throwing it back heavily, and glared out into the night.

His eyes fell upon the figure of a young man huddled in the doorway, cold and wet, and shivering violently. The tension which had marked the landlord's features a moment before fell away and was replaced by a look of surprise and concern. He ushered the grateful stranger inside and seated him before the now extinguished fire. His wife entered; she approached gingerly, looking uncertainly at the stranger.

'You'd best make up the fire again, Mary; I'll fetch some brandy.' Soon the visitor, with the brandy warming his veins, was sufficiently revived to express his gratitude to the couple.

'I am sorry to put you to so much trouble,' said he. 'I was on my way to meet my friends in C_, when the snow came down and the fog got so heavy I became hopelessly lost. When night fell I lost all hope of salvation. When I saw the lights of your inn I gave a prayer of thanks and made for them with all the strength I had left.'

The landlord looked into the face of the young stranger. The man's skin was as white as the snow, which still clung in places to his hat and coat, and his lips had a strange, bluish grey coldness about them.

'Yes,' said the landlord, 'when the snow comes in these parts it comes fast, and it's as easy for a man who's lived here all his days to lose his way as it is for a stranger to do so.'

'Do you have any rooms free at present?' asked the stranger. 'If not, I should be grateful for the shelter of a stable or…' The landlord waved a dismissive hand.

'No, no,' said he, 'we have room enough. But first, we must get you warmed and fed, for, if you'll forgive my saying so, sir, there is a terrible pallor about you, and you don't look at all well.'

'Thank you; you are most kind. It is true; I do not feel quite well. I fear it was a near thing for me tonight.'

'I think it best that we send for the doctor, if necessary, at first light; we haven't a hope of reaching him tonight.'

Soon the stranger was wrapped up in heavy blankets before a roaring fire, his feeble fingers wrapped around a bowl of steaming stew.

'In my relief at finding you, I'm afraid I forgot to introduce myself; my name is Turner.'

'Robinson, sir, and this good lady, as you must have gathered, is my wife.'

'Well, I am heartily glad to meet you both.' He paused for a moment to partake of another mouthful of stew. 'I hope I did not disturb your household too greatly. I was so afraid you would not hear me that I must have knocked loudly enough to wake the dead.' A little gasp escaped the landlord's wife as the poker she had been holding fell with a loud clatter on the stone floor. The sound echoed in the silence of the night. She turned away so that they would not see her face. The landlord threw a glance towards her.

'There now, Mary.'

'Is something wrong? I hope I have said nothing amiss,' inquired the stranger, looking from one to the other of his hosts.

'The truth is, sir,' said the landlord hesitantly, 'your coming here, as you did tonight, gave us something of a fright, you might say.'

'A fright?'

'It was the knocking! That terrible knocking,' cried the woman, her hand instantly at her mouth in a vain attempt to halt the words.

'There now, Mary, don't take on so,' soothed her husband.

'The fact is, sir, when we heard you banging at the door like that, well, we thought you were...,' he paused, then went on weakly, 'someone else.' The young man's eyes were wide.

'Oh,' said he, 'and who is that, if you do not mind my asking?'

'Well, that is the very thing which I myself would like to know, sir, for we have no notion of it.' The woman shook her head wildly.

'No, no I don't want to know.'

'I'm afraid I don't follow,' said the stranger.

The landlord pulled up a chair and seated himself opposite his guest. He leaned forward, the light of the fire casting shadows on his rugged face.

'It's like this you see, every night for the past week, always about the hour you came to us, we have been disturbed by such a banging at the door as you yourself were making. Three rounds of three knocks. I've never managed to catch anyone hanging about the place. We don't have any particularly close neighbours here, and there was no time for anyone to conceal themselves. The cause is a mystery, and I'm afraid the whole business has been playing on my wife's nerves, and I can't say mine are the better for it.'

'The three knocks of death.' In the stillness of the night, the hushed words hung in the air between them.

'What is that?' asked the stranger.

'A foolish superstition, nothing more,' the landlord replied firmly.

'Is it?' the woman turned on her husband. 'Are you so sure?' The stranger looked bewildered and a little uncomfortable. The woman watched him narrowly. 'Around these parts, said she, 'they say knocking like that means death is coming. You may call it superstition if you like, but those tales don't survive so long without there being some truth to them.' The young man looked uncertainly at the landlord.

'Well, I cannot speak for your previous disturbances,' said he, 'but tonight at least you have an explanation for the knocking.'

'Just so,' replied the landlord.

They remained in silence until, his meal over, the stranger was shown to his room. As soon as they had shut themselves into their own room for the night, Mrs Robinson spoke urgently to her husband.

'I don't like it, Bill. There's something about that young man.'

'Now, Mary, what cause have you to distrust the man?'

'The knocking; the knocking brings death in its wake, and tonight it brought him.' Her husband opened his mouth in mute protest, but she plunged on. 'No, Bill I don't like it, and I'll be happier when that fellow is out from under our roof.'

'Surely you wouldn't have me put him out?' asked he in astonishment.

'Of course not! What do you take me for, Bill Robinson? I'd never dream of such a thing! But still, I'll be happier once the doctor has seen him and he's on his way.'

'What is it that you fear, Mary,' said her husband softly, 'surely not violence? Anyone can see that his weakness and exhaustion are real enough poor fellow.'

'I don't know, but I am not easy in my mind; that's all I do know.'

'Well, let us sleep now and hope that the morning sets your fears to flight.'

It was a restless night for that good lady. She lay awake, listening to the sounds of the night, alert to every noise within the old inn, the creaking of the ageing timbers and the sighing of the wind in the chimneys. She was conscious every moment of a feeling of expectation, though what it was she was waiting for she did not know.

The morning came on slowly, but with its light, the shadows of the night were swept away, and the couple arose to face a new day. The snow had stopped during the night, and the world outside shimmered, white with snow and frost. The bare branches of the trees glistened, as though hung with diamonds.

The landlord, feeling it best before calling out the doctor, went to look in upon his unfortunate visitor. He knocked on the door but no answer came. Again he knocked, again no answer. Thinking the young man, exhausted from his adventures, might be sleeping still, he knocked once more; no sound came from within. He was growing concerned for the young man's safety. He turned the handle of the door; it was unlocked. He pushed it open slightly and peered into the room.

Ordinarily, he would not have taken such a liberty, but, given the circumstances, he thought it for the best.

He blinked, his eyes taking in every inch of the room; it was empty. The bed was undisturbed, and there was no sign of either the stranger or his few possessions. His first thought was that he had slipped out in the night, but to what end? Where could he go in such weather? Had he then taken flight in the morning to avoid any financial obligation he might be put to? It did not seem likely. On examination he found the inn door to still be locked and bolted on the inside; no windows were open and none of the handful of other guests had seen the young man. Where then had he gone and how? He did not have time to dwell further on the matter at that moment, for his duties pressed, and it was not until much later that he had time to think upon the strangeness of the situation.

***

That evening, a few of the local men, who had braved the snow drifts, were gathered before the fire in the bar, ruminating on the winters of their childhoods. The general consensus amongst the elder of their number was that the younger had never seen a real winter, not like the ones they had experienced; now, those were real winters and so forth. The landlord listened and contributed with his customary good humour. It was during these reminiscences that one of the patrons recalled an incident on a night such as the one just passed.

'Do you remember,' said he, 'must have been five, or was it six, years past, during old Godwin's time as landlord? No, I'm a liar; it was more like eight. A bitter night it was. You couldn't see two feet in front of you for the snow and the fog, bitter, frozen fog. Come the morning, they found the body of some poor soul out there on the hillside. Seems the poor lad was travelling on to the town when the weather turned, and he got lost. The worst of it was that he was so near to the inn when they found him. A few more feet and it might have been his salvation.' A memory stirred in the back of the landlord's mind.

'Yes, I remember hearing something of it now. A young fellow wasn't it? Though I can't recall his name.' A vague uneasiness was settling on the landlord. From the corner of his eye, he saw a shape in the doorway; his wife had appeared and had evidently been listening with great attention to the men's conversation. The old orator chewed on his pipe and thought for a moment.

'Turner, yes that was it. Old Turner's lad from over S_ way; come to spend a few days with friends before Christmas. Poor lad never saw another Christmas. If you were to go up that hill there, just beyond the old oak tree, you'd see a stone to his memory. Of course, he isn't buried there mind, but some of us thought it right there should be some memorial to the lad there, poor soul.'

The subject changed, and no further mention was made of the young man by either the landlord or his wife that night, yet both were thinking of him.

That Christmas Eve, on their way home from church, the couple's way took them past the stone on the hill. On that spot, they laid a wreath of evergreen and spent a moment in silent prayer for the young man for whom their help had come too late. Hand in hand, they turned away and made their way homeward, across the snow-covered hills, towards the inn and Christmas Day.

A Spirited Evening

The rain beat down hard on the side of the cab as he stepped down. His coat collar was turned up to protect him from the driving elements, but still the wind forced the icy downpour into the hardened features of his face. His cheeks were red, raw from the relentless rain and cold. His nose too was red, but that resulted from a warmer source, something to keep the cold out. He smiled grimly, reflecting that it was the only spirit he was likely to see that night.

He made his way to the door and pulled on the bell. It was a foul night and unseasonable too. Spring should have been insinuating itself into the air and the landscape by now. Instead, the remnants of winter were clinging on, reluctant to relinquish their power over men.

What the deuce was taking so long? Did they expect him to stand there all night, to catch his death? Perhaps they were trying to increase their clientèle. He allowed himself the briefest of smiles; an unpleasant smile it was too. He rang the bell again impatiently. The sound of hurrying footsteps was heard within. *At last.* The wind moaned around his ears; for a moment he imagined he heard a whisper carried on it. It was ridiculous of course. How could a whisper, if anyone were there to whisper, be heard above that cacophony? A flash of lightning lighted the street in a depressing, dingy tableau.

The door finally swung open, and he pushed his way past the apologetic young maid and stood dripping in the hallway.

'This is a fine way to treat guests, I must say, leaving them to catch their deaths on the doorstep. I rang the bell twice, girl; what kept you?' She cast an eye over the soggy visitor. The look was not without a trace of disdain.

'I am terribly sorry, sir,' said she, taking his hat and coat. 'The storm must have covered the sound of the bell.'

'Very well,' said he, some of his ill temper subsiding now that he was on the right side of the door. 'Lead the way.'

'Just through here, sir.' She led him through the door on the right of the hall, which opened into a good sized sitting room. It was dimly lit. A round table had been placed in the centre of the room, which was presently unoccupied. He took out his watch; he was a little before his time. The other guests would be here shortly.

'The mistress will be along directly, sir; she is still preparing herself,' said the little maid. He nodded curtly and responded in the negative to the girl's offer of refreshment. He wanted a clear head for the business before him. She gave him one last brief, appraising look, then bobbed and exited the room.

He looked about him. Several sheets of paper had been placed carefully on the table, with a slim lead pencil beside them. A wicker ball and a small bell were also in readiness; he examined each in turn. Finding nothing, he began to prowl the room. He occupied himself with looking behind curtains and peering into objects on the mantelpiece. He sniffed the air; no scent of flowers at any rate. He hoped this one wasn't inclined towards materialising wet flowers over her sitters. Twice he had been drenched in that way. It seemed to him that these spirits took some great pleasure in dampening his.

He found no hidden alcoves in which to hide apports, no vases of flowers, no obvious trap door in the ceiling. No hidden wires were found which might cause objects to fly from their places. He turned his attention back to the table. He gave the bell and the ball a final cursory examination.

Either this one was very careless in leaving him alone in the séance room or she was confident enough in her means of deception that she felt she was in no peril from him; no doubt he'd soon remove that confidence. Perhaps her tools of the trade would be brought in with her. He would make a point of keeping a close eye out for confederates, like the maid. He might catch her in some deception whilst the medium was supposed to be holding his attention. It wouldn't be the first time someone had attempted to fool him in that way.

'I trust everything is to your satisfaction?' inquired a voice behind him. Startled, he almost dropped the ball. Cursing silently, he turned around to see Mrs Hopper, the medium, standing in the doorway, wearing a half-smile, one eyebrow arched. He eyed her coldly. He was annoyed with himself; it wasn't like him to be caught unawares, and he resented it. He was vexed too with the calm, composed confidence - or was it arrogance? - of her demeanour. He was going to enjoy exposing her, even if it meant a second visit.

Sometimes it was necessary to see the phenomena first before you could trace the origin of the illusion, for such it must always be. Some mediums were more creative than others, granted, but all who came before him were exposed for the charlatans they were, eventually. In spiritualist circles, his name was feared and loathed in equal measure. It was a reputation he thoroughly enjoyed.

As the medium swept into the room, the maid returned with a second guest. She was a rather pathetic looking, damp-eyed, middle-aged woman called Waverley. Her every movement, her every word, had the air of an apology.

Another credulous example of the modern woman. Probably grieving for a dear departed mother or maiden aunt, he thought to himself. IIe felt no sympathy; he never did. He wagered her husband didn't either; if the departed was anything like the wife, he was probably glad to be free of her.

She was followed by the final guest, a rather shamefaced looking old gentleman by the name of Warburton, who was possessed of the most magnificent example of a moustache he had ever seen; it was magnificent, not least of all, because it detracted so much from the rest of the man's features, which he observed were not handsome and had little to commend them.

As they were seated, and the tedious formalities of the introductions were concluded, he paid close attention to the maid, who was lighting the candles on the table. He watched the medium, satisfying himself that her hands never moved from their position on the table. He studied the other guests, one or both of whom could be confederates in this charade; he doubted it. He didn't think it likely that either of them had the intelligence to carry out any form of deception. In fact, they looked pathologically honest. He sneered at the thought; he had never considered honesty to be a very desirable virtue.

Mrs Hopper placed the matches on the table next to her. The maid blew out the candles in the rest of the room and took up her position at the table. He made sure he was sitting next to Mrs Hopper so that he could be sure that at least one of her hands was not free to produce any manifestation during the hand-holding business. He wondered peevishly why it was that spirits should be so disinclined to play their tricks in a well-lit room. The candles flickered. The pale light illuminated the faces of his fellow sitters in a watery glow. The shadows seemed to shift strangely about them.

As he gazed at the candles the darkness around him closed in. The storm raged outside; at a rumble of thunder, he heard Mrs Waverley give a little gasp. He rolled his eyes impatiently. The mousey woman was likely to have a fit of hysterics at the first of Mrs Hopper's parlour tricks. If a little thunder troubled her, how did she imagine she would deal with the spirits of the dead talking to her?

Mrs Hopper took up the pencil and laid it upon a piece of paper.

'I will begin by putting myself into a trance, during which any spirit present may use me in order to produce any pictures or messages they may wish to share.' He yawned; the mousey woman cast him a reproachful look. He returned her gaze with a cold indifference, and she looked away again. *Scurry back to your hole, little mouse.*

Mrs Hopper took a few deep breaths; he listened as her breathing became shallower and shallower. Her eyes closed gently. For a few moments nothing happened; then the pencil began to move, slowly at first then making rapid progress along the paper. He could see a word forming.

"Murderer"

For a brief moment, he felt alarm flare in his chest; this was not the usual sort of message. He soon recovered himself, however. She was just trying to scare these gullible fools. He had no reason to concern himself. He was irritated with himself for being so on edge; it wasn't like him. He felt as though his nerves were out of order tonight. Perhaps he was coming down with some malady. The pencil began to move again.

"I will come to you... midnight tonight."

Everyone around the table turned suspicious looks upon each other. He refused to be drawn by such blatant nonsense. Then the mousey looking Mrs Waverley spoke up.

'What is your name, spirit?' she asked tentatively. The reply came.

"V.G."

Confusion, and not a little alarm, passed over the faces of the sitters. The mousey woman threw him a momentary look and then averted her eyes again, as though it disgusted her to look upon him. His mouth felt suddenly dry. It was a cheap trick designed to unnerve the credulous, of course. He knew that and yet...and yet. He was seized, despite himself, with an uncomfortable sensation. Could this woman, Mrs Hopper, suspect something? No, such a thing was unthinkable; he had been too careful for that.

The air felt somehow heavier, thick and oppressive. At that moment, Mrs Hopper came out of her trance, smiling happily. She saw the looks upon the faces around the table and, with a slight frown, studied the words on the paper.

'How extraordinary!' she exclaimed. 'Does this mean anything to anyone here?'

There was silence. She could hardly suppose they would confess it if it did, he thought. He certainly wouldn't.

'Well, dear me that is very odd,' she continued. 'I've never had a message like that before; it's usually a matter of, "I am at peace; do not grieve for me", etc., etc. Well, really I don't quite know what to do. I do not know if it is wise to continue.' There was a murmur of protest from Mrs Waverley. 'Very well, perhaps we should continue; it may just be some mischievous spirit playing tricks with us. Let us see; we may shed some light on things yet.'

The thought occurred to him that he would much rather she did not shed light on things. He pushed the thought aside, though he did not feel so sure of himself as previously. This was nothing he hadn't seen before; why should reason fail him now?

They were instructed to hold hands, to form a spirit circle; He took her hand and hoped that she would not detect the slight tremor in his. After a few moments spent in reaching the appropriate state to commune with the spirits, she began.

Nothing happened; he began to feel a sense of relief, but then...

'I have a message for Matilda. There is a woman, an elderly lady; she says she loves you. She watches over you...,' she coughed, 'and your husband. Do not be concerned for her; she is at peace.'

Mrs Waverley, whose eyes were even more teary than before, gave a little gesture of pleasure.

A message followed for the old gentleman along the same lines, but this time from a departed sister, the usual nonsense.

'Are there any other spirits who wish to make themselves known?' asked the medium. 'Speak to us.' Silence..., and then the bell began to ring. He could have sworn he had heard it before it began to move. Then the ball began to roll steadily around the table, coming to a stop before him. It stayed there for a moment. It seemed to him to be quivering, pulsating somehow. Then, without warning the ball flew from the table and over his head, narrowly missing him as he dived out of the way. The ball crashed into a vase on the mantelpiece behind him. The vase shattered, scattering fragments of pottery across the floor.

'Oh! Now really, that is very vexing,' cried Mrs Hopper. 'I was really rather fond of that vase, but there you are; I suppose it was my own fault for putting it in this room; I really should have known better. It seems the spirits are a little out of temper this evening. Perhaps it is best if we do call an end to proceedings. I am very sorry to cut things so short, but we are all subject to the whims of the spirits you know.' That notion made him feel distinctly uncomfortable. 'Light the candles, Jane, and bring me some water, there's a good girl.'

As the girl began to rise, she turned suddenly pale and slumped forward in her seat. Nobody moved; then one by one the others followed suit. They all lay insensible in their seats, all but him. Mrs Hopper sat suddenly upright, her eyes fixed on him, and she spoke, but it was not her voice that he heard. Yet it was a voice he knew. Equally, he knew that what he was hearing was not possible, he was delusional, dreaming, insane! What other explanation could there be?

'You thought to be rid of me! Did you really think it would be so easy?' demanded the accusing voice. He felt ill. He fought to maintain consciousness as a wave of nausea welled up within him. The maid turned to him and with the same voice said,

'You think that you've won? That you can escape? There is no escape. I will be avenged!' This last remark was spat at him with vitriolic rage. Then to his horror, every face at the table turned to him with the same accusing eyes and with the same voice, her voice, they laughed in unison, a laugh so malicious and hate-filled as to shake a man to his bones. Then, the spell broken, the company blinked and looked about them in bewilderment.

'I feel very peculiar,' said the teary-eyed Mrs Waverley.

'I think something may have occurred,' said Mrs Hopper weakly. 'Does anyone recall anything?' He remained silent, not trusting himself to speak. They looked from one to the other of their fellows; no one gave any indication that they were aware of what had passed. His hands were sweating. He fancied that the medium's eyes rested on him a fraction longer than on the others. He longed to be out of that hateful house.

'Well then, there's no harm done, and we are none of us the worse for our experiences I trust?' She smiled warmly, and the mood seemed to lift from them.

Soon the neat little sitting room was illuminated in the glow of candles and oil lamps; but for all that, the company were not entirely cheerful. The maid brought her mistress the water that she'd requested and then went forth to retrieve coats and hats. Mrs Hopper rubbed her temples and sipped delicately at the water.

'Perhaps something a little stronger may be in order this evening,' she mumbled to herself.

The other sitters went out first; as he reached the threshold, Mrs Hopper put a hand on his arm. He turned and saw her looking upon him with a very curious expression.

'Take care, Mr Gains,' said she. He shook her off angrily and stormed out into the night.

The rain had stopped by this time, so he decided he would walk home. The air of the séance room had made him feel stifled and light headed. He turned his head upwards allowing his face to feel the night breeze; it refreshed him a little. She had rattled him; he could not deny it, at least to himself. How could she know? Not a living soul knew his secret; those words came back to him, *not a living soul.* Were they all in on it? How else could he explain what had happened? He could not allow himself to believe that what he had experienced was real. It was all some absurd conspiracy against him! As a cloud drifted across the moon, he jumped at a shadow in an alleyway; for a moment he had mistaken it for the figure of a woman.

He was tired; he needed to sleep. He was to call on his fiancée in the morning, and he couldn't present himself in the condition he was in now. He hoped no word of the night's dealings would reach her. The last thing he needed was his carefully laid plans being ruined because she took fright. Not that he thought it likely; she was utterly in his power.

Whatever evidence you placed before her, she would not be parted from him; he felt sure. She would believe anything he told her. She was just the kind of woman he needed now, young, pretty, pliable, and above all, rich.

There was no longer anything standing in his way; he was free to marry, and what a prize he had caught.

On his return, shortly before 11 pm, he decided to go straight to bed. A good night's rest and the horrors of that vile room would be dispelled, or so he hoped.

Time passed, and midnight rolled around. As the clock in the hall struck the hour, he awoke with a start. In that instant, he recalled with growing disquiet the words spelt out by the medium.

"I will come to you...midnight tonight."

He became aware of a sound, gentle at first then growing more insistent. Someone was rattling the doorknob. He saw it shudder, then begin to turn slowly. He held his breath, motionless with terror. There was a creaking sound as the door edged slowly open, as though to prolong his suffering; then with a sudden crash, the door was thrown back to its full extent. A dismal cry echoed through the night.

***

Mrs Hopper placed the newspaper down on the breakfast table.

'Well, Jane, it seems our Mr Gains won't be calling on us again.'

'No, madam.'

'It must have been quite a shock for his poor fiancée. Still...,' she paused, looking thoughtfully at the paper, 'perhaps it may be, after all, for the best.' Jane nodded solemnly. They remained in silence for a few moments until Mrs Hopper asked,

'What was his late wife's name? I cannot quite recall it.'

'I believe Mrs Gains's name was Violet, madam.'

'Ah yes of course,' said she gravely. She nodded. 'They say the poor man appears to have died of fright. I wonder what can have frightened him so.' The two women exchanged a look. Jane shivered ever so slightly. It was clear that neither of the women wished to dwell on what could have frightened Mr Gains into his grave. So it was that, by silent consent, Mr Gains was never spoken of again in the house of Mrs Hopper

The Darkness Within

The small town of Market Stoneborough is a quaint and rather picturesque example of its type. The inhabitants are genial and friendly, and the streets are lined with attractive, welcoming little shops, neatly kept and dutifully tended, which can easily satisfy the wants of most visitors. The town itself is surrounded by a wide and open expanse of countryside, which offers the prospect of a pleasant afternoon's walk to those inclined toward exercise. It is altogether a most comfortable and commodious place in which to dwell.

It is, in fact, a town so like hundreds of others of the kind as to be wholly unremarkable; not at all the place you would expect to find anything in the least extraordinary, or shall we say mysterious.

Yet, if you were to turn your steps in the direction of one of the less well-trodden alleys of the town, to one which runs just behind the church and opens immediately after the old Royal Oak Inn, you would find a bookshop; in that bookshop you would find a man by the name of

Mr Jabez Worthington. In the figure of that jovial and good-natured proprietor, there is little to suggest anything of an extraordinary nature, but Mr Worthington is a man to whom extraordinary things have happened. He could, if called upon to do so, tell a very curious tale, the tale which I shall now relate.

It happened that Mr Worthington was in the habit of purchasing, from time to time, certain volumes from sale houses with which to supplement his inventory, as well as his own personal collection. At one such sale, he managed to obtain, at a modest price, a small assortment of books lately in the collection of a local scholar who was now deceased. The books were delivered on the morning following the sale; however, not until the evening, when the day's business was concluded and he was alone, did he have the opportunity of examining his purchases more closely.

Before the fire, in the cosy little sitting room above the shop, under the watchful eye of his cat, he began the task of checking and sorting the books. This was a task he always enjoyed, for books were his passion as well as his livelihood. Indeed, he might have been a richer man, financially at least, if he had not been so fond of increasing his own collection. The dusty smell of books, long unopened, filled the air as he leafed casually through the pages. There were a few general items of some local interest and some rarer volumes, which he knew would be of interest to one or two of his regular clients.

'Hello!' cried he suddenly. 'What's this?' He was turning one of the books over in his hands and examining it minutely. His cat looked up at him quizzically. Dropping softly from the armchair, she padded over to him. She leapt up on the little table, perching herself precariously atop a pile of books.

'What have we here, old girl?' he mused, absent-mindedly stroking the creature. 'This book seems rather heavy for its size, and see here, there's a lock on it. I wonder if it's a diary or something of the sort; perhaps it was put into the sale in error. But then it does have a title on the binding, "*The Darkness Within*". Well, dear me, it isn't a very cheerful title is it?' The cat tilted her head in acknowledgement and blinked non-committally.

'It is strange, but I do not remember seeing it at the saleroom; I suppose I must have missed it in my haste to get the particular items on which you are so happily sitting.' He picked up the cat and put her gently on the floor. 'Well, I had best check with the saleroom before I make any attempt upon the lock at any rate.'

He placed the book down on the table and picked up another volume. Seating himself before the fire with a glass of port, he began to read. The cat watched him for a moment, then leapt back up onto the table and resumed her place. She yawned lazily and began to groom herself. Suddenly her ears pricked up; something had caught her attention. She gazed intently at the strange book; stretching her nose towards it, she sniffed it delicately. Upon the instant, she was more alert. She sat upright and gave the book a testing little tap with her paw. She meowed and again tapped the book, harder this time. She was up on all fours, her back arched and her fur bristling. She hissed loudly and began to claw at the book, knocking it to the floor as she did so.

'My word, Cleopatra! Whatever has gotten into you?' Mr Worthington leapt from his chair with a start.

Removing the protesting cat from the table, not without a scratch or two to show for it, he picked up the book and examined it narrowly. 'Well, you naughty girl, you don't seem to have caused too much damage.' Cleopatra whined loudly, gave him an indignant look and curled up before the fire. 'I had better put this out of harm's way, as you seem to have taken such a dislike to it.' He placed the book carefully in his writing desk and locked the drawer.

There it remained until Mr Worthington, having received assurances that the book was indeed part of the assortment of books he had purchased and that there had been no key provided, retrieved it. This time he took the precaution of putting Cleopatra out first. He was just standing at his counter, wondering how best to go about removing the lock, when the door swung open, clattering the bell noisily, and a very flustered man called out,

'Mr Worthington, I really must insist that you do not open that book.' Mr Worthington was astonished; his blank expression proclaimed as much, for the other man, removing his hat, made haste to explain himself.

'I am sorry to startle you, sir, but I had to stop you opening the book.'

'Why, whatever for? What can it have to do with you?'

'Just this, I am Mr Julius Cartwright, son of the late Nathaniel Cartwright, the former owner of that book.'

'Ah, I see.' Worthington's face clouded over. 'Or rather I do not see. You say I must not open the book, but you do not say why.'

'I'm afraid the book was included in the sale in error. I was away at the time, and I left an agent in charge of making the arrangements. Somehow, I can't imagine how, the book ended up in the books to be sold rather than those which were to go to storage. I was very clear that it should not be sold. My father left me all his books, which I was to dispose of or keep as I saw fit; however, he made me promise that I would not sell this particular volume nor should I suffer it to be opened. There was no stipulation of this in his will; he said that he did not wish to draw undue attention to the book in case it should entice someone to break in upon its secrets. So, although

I have no legal obligation I do have a moral one, to obey my father's final wish.'

'Well, dear me that is a curious tale.'

'I know that it sounds quite mad; I have always assumed it was some sort of diary; in which case, why he did not order me to burn it if he feared it being read I cannot imagine. Well, there it is, sir. You have purchased the book and I cannot compel you to return it, but I will of course recompense you handsomely should you be willing to do so.'

'Not at all, my dear sir, of course you shall have it.'

'You are very good, sir; I thank you.'

During this exchange, neither man had noticed Cleopatra slip in through the open door. Seeing the book on the counter she suddenly gave a cry and pounced on it, worrying at it with her teeth and claws. Taken aback by the sudden ferocity of the animal, neither man moved. The book fell heavily to the ground. Mr Worthington roused himself suddenly and removed the animal from the room. Having closed the door on her, he turned his attention to the book.

Both men stared in mute bewilderment; the book lay open on the floor, the lock broken beside it. Between the covers, the pages had been hollowed out. The opening that had been created contained a small walnut box. It was decorated with grotesque and diabolical figures, some dancing and some leering savagely. It was inlaid too, with a black metallic looking material, yet it was not like any metal they had ever seen.

'Good heavens!' cried Mr Worthington. 'No wonder it was so heavy.'

'I do not understand what this means,' said Cartwright falteringly. Worthington bent forward, hampered rather by his rotund stature, to examine the box. He picked it up gingerly and turned it over in his hands.

'It seems to be locked.' Suddenly he gave a cry of pain and dropped the box on the counter. 'I say, it scratched my hand. The corner on the thing is devilishly sharp; see here, it has drawn blood.' He held out his left hand, which bore traces of blood on the palm.

'Hello!' cried Cartwright with great excitement. 'What's this?' he was leaning over the counter and peering, beneath furrowed brows, at the box. He pointed to the inlay. Worthington saw at once what had alarmed him; the metallic substance had changed colour; instead of black, it was now red, blood red.

'Whatever can be the meaning of it?'

'I do not know. It is very singular.'

'I don't like this.'

'Nor do I,' said Cartwright.

'What should we do?' asked Worthington, dabbing at his forehead with his handkerchief.

'I don't know; I have never seen anything like it, and I do not trust it,' said Cartwright, drumming his fingers on the counter. 'My father must have had a good reason for wishing the box to be kept hidden. I do not think it would be wise for us to try and open it, and yet whatever is inside may have some bearing on the matter.'

'Cleopatra certainly doesn't care for it.'

'I'm sorry?' He shook his head slightly, his confusion evident.

'My cat,' said Worthington apologetically.

'Ah, yes, indeed. I have heard it said that animals are sensitive to certain things that we are not.'

'But what are we to do?' asked Worthington imploringly. 'I cannot help but feel that something has been set in motion here.' He gazed at his injured hand; it ached abominably. He swallowed.

'I feel it too,' whispered Cartwright. 'I think the best thing we can do for the moment is to lock the thing away somewhere safe until we know a little more.'

'Agreed.'

'Then, if you have no objection, I shall take it with me. I shall lock it in my safe; no one can interfere with it there.'

'I have no objection.' In truth he was glad not to have to spend a night with the thing in the house; it disgusted him rather. Cartwright picked up the box, with some trepidation, placed it back into the book and left the shop with promises to return on the morrow.

***

It was a poor night's rest for Mr Worthington. His hand throbbed, and his sleep was plagued by nightmares. Once he awoke to the sound of voices, screaming as though in torment. Black shapes seemed to fill the room, and he had the strange sensation that he was not alone.

Around a quarter past three in the morning, he was awoken again, this time by someone knocking at the door downstairs. Eyelids heavy, and dressing gown trailing, he stumbled, by the light of his bedside candle, to the door.

'Who's there? What do you mean making such a noise at this hour?' he demanded irritably. No answer came. He opened the door a sliver and peered out into the darkness of the early morning. He saw no one. He was about to slam the door in annoyance when, by the pale light of his candle, he saw something on the doorstep. Cautiously, he opened the door to its full extent. He looked down at the doorstep to see the box.

He blinked uncomprehendingly. How could this be? Was it some sort of trick on the part of Cartwright? He doubted it; the man seemed honest, and besides what purpose could there be in playing such a trick? He could not simply leave the box where it was, and yet he was loath to touch it again.

Reaching into his dressing gown pocket, he felt for his handkerchief; he pulled it out, and using it to shield his hand he picked the box up gently. He found, to his utter revulsion, that the figures he had noted earlier appeared even more ghastly by candlelight; they seemed to glare spitefully at him, with sinister purpose. He locked it away in his desk and returned to bed, resolving to call on Cartwright first thing after breakfast.

Oh, how far off did that dawn seem; with his eyes closed sleeplessly against the night, he felt the hours trickle slowly by. He could not sleep, though he was tired enough. Whenever sleep seemed close he felt himself brought back to consciousness by the distant sound of voices whispering to him. Yet no words could he discern.

He became convinced that the source of the sound was within the house. He could hear Cleopatra whining downstairs; she too was troubled. Rising from his bed he tiptoed cautiously through the house, his senses alert for any sound or movement, trying to discern the source of the disturbance, all the while fearing an attack upon his life.

His quest led him to his sitting room. He pushed the door back as slowly as he dared. The room was empty. The realisation dawned slowly and painfully on him that the sound was emanating from within the desk. For a moment he did not move; then, muttering an oath and bidding his protesting feet forwards, he approached the desk. Leaning forward awkwardly, he listened with great attention; sure enough, there were voices coming from the desk.

Hardly trusting his judgement, he stretched out his shaking hand to unlock the desk. The key slipped in his damp fingers as he struggled to manoeuvre it. Finally, it turned and he heard the click of the lock. Summoning all the courage he had left to him, he opened the desk.

The noise from within increased a little as he peered in upon the box, though he could still make no sense of the whispered words. He stayed only long enough to establish that the sound was indeed coming from within the box. He scrambled to secure the desk once more and then rushed headlong up the stairs to his room. He was closely followed by Cleopatra, who almost tripped him up in her haste to get away.

He spent the night clinging to his bedclothes, in a fearful vigil. When the dawn finally crawled feebly through the window of his room it found him a frailer and older looking man than it had done the day before.

After he had dressed, he went straightaway to his sitting room. Unlocking his desk, he peered inside to reassure himself that the box was indeed there and he had not been subject to some horrific dream; it was there, exactly where he had left it. It was as he had feared.

Over breakfast he examined the box minutely, not touching it any more than necessary. The daylight had made him braver but no less cautious. He mistrusted it, and his further examination of it had done nothing to dispel his dislike of the object; the voices had now stopped at least, or he would not have been so bold. The sooner he had returned the loathsome thing to Cartwright the better.

***

No one, except perhaps Mr Worthington himself, could have been more astounded than Cartwright to learn that the box no longer resided in his safe, to which he had committed it the day before. In point of fact, his first action upon seeing the box in Worthington's possession was immediately to examine the safe. He wished to satisfy himself that it really was gone and there was no possibility of a duplicate. As you may suppose, the safe was empty of its charge, though the book remained.

Cartwright was even more perturbed when Worthington related his adventures of the night to him. He did not for a moment doubt the other man's tale, for he too felt that immense dislike for the box.

What then were these two gentlemen to do? An object that could disappear from a locked safe only to rematerialize on the other side of town was a quandary to be sure. Clearly, to place it under lock and key was of no use now. Yet, Cartwright reflected, it had lain harmlessly amongst his father's possessions for years and caused no mischief; what then could have provoked it? What had changed? His gaze fell heavily on Worthington. He shivered but gave no voice to the thought which was now in his mind. He feared for that gentleman.

It was decided that Worthington would return to attend to his business, committing the care of the mysterious box once more to Cartwright. Cartwright, for his part, was to continue the examination of the box and his father's papers, in the hope of finding some reference or clue to the object's provenance.

Alas, his search proved fruitless, and by the drawing of the evening, he was no nearer a solution to the problem than he had been in the morning. At last, as the shadows closed in around him, his head began to droop as he fought the heaviness in his eyelids.

'Help me, father,' he whispered. 'Tell me what to do.' The papers that he had been reading fell in a scattered heap upon the floor. He slumped in his chair, as sleep overtook him, and he drifted into a fitful doze. Time passed, and something in the atmosphere of the room shifted. His eyes began to flicker.

***

Mr Worthington, having been deprived of his previous night's sleep, was ready to retire all the earlier that evening. Though he was not easy in his mind, he found sleep came, nonetheless. But, as though in anticipation of the event, he again awoke a little after three and found himself listening sharply to the silence in the room. Then, it came again, the same knocking. This time, though he was no less disturbed, he was at least less surprised. With an air of resignation, he threw his dressing gown about him and went downstairs.

Sure enough, he found the box, just as he had done on the previous night. This time it was with something akin to irritation that he snatched up the box and took it indoors. He did not, however, place it in his desk, as he had done before. For reasons he himself could not explain, were he called upon to do so, he placed the box on a chest of draws in his room and went back to bed.

There was little chance of sleep, however, for the moment he closed his eyes there came once again that persistent whispering. Though not conscious of having moved, he found himself standing beside the box. The voices within seemed to urge him to action. He found that the words, though no less obscure, seemed now to reach into his mind, to find some common understanding. They spoke to something in him, something primal and long forgotten in his human heart.

'Open it,' they seemed to say. 'Behold the wonders it contains. Free us, and you shall have such rewards as mortal man has never seen.'

His finger stretched out towards the lid of the box. He felt the absolute conviction that this time it would open to his touch if he would but try. His fingers brushed lightly against the wood. He may well have given in to that strange impulse if it had not been for the peculiar sensation which greeted his fingers; as his touch lighted upon the painted figures they seemed to move and writhe beneath his fingertips. Withdrawing in sudden alarm, he came abruptly to his senses. What horror had he been so near to unleashing? He made up his mind at once. At first light, he would set out again to call upon Cartwright.

True to his intention, he was at Cartwright's door before the sun's rays had fully chased away the gloom of the desolate night. There was some confusion, and not a little surprise, on the part of the servants to find a dishevelled guest thrust upon them at such an hour; it was not long, however, before an equally dishevelled Cartwright appeared.

'Good heavens, Worthington, it seems you have had no better night than I!'

'Indeed, I have much to tell you. But you say you have also been...troubled?'

'I have; I confess I have passed no easy night.'

'What then has occurred?'

'I was visited by my father.' Worthington stared, his jaw dropping slackly.

'I beg your pardon?'

'I do not know whether you would call it a vision or a dream, but I saw him as clearly as I see you, and he was as real as you are.' He tapped the other man on the shoulder with a long finger, as though to reassure himself of the reality of Mr Worthington. 'In the dream, or vision if you will, he seemed to be unable to speak to me, yet he was in a desperate state to communicate something to me.

'He led me to a lake, out in the woods behind the house, where you were waiting for us. He pointed towards you, and I saw that your hand was dripping with blood; in your other hand, you held the box. Then he turned and looked at me narrowly, as though to be sure I had understood him. Then, some invisible force seemed to tear him away, and I was instantly awake.'

'Is this Lake far from here?'

'The place is not far; I recognized it very clearly, and yet there is no lake on that spot; there is just a clearing.' There was silence as both men thought on this. 'But you were going to tell me of your own disturbance,' said Cartwright after a moment.

Worthington explained, as clearly as he could, what had befallen him and of the strange desire which had come upon him to look within the box. Cartwright's face darkened.

'It seems to me that the abominable object has formed some connection to you. I suspect something happened that day when you cut your hand on the thing.'

'It is too ghastly to contemplate. We must do something, for I am afraid of what will happen if it should succeed in its persuasions!'

'We must go to that spot which my father showed to me and see what happens. I can see no other course.'

'Nor I,' said Worthington resignedly.

'Then let us go now; there is no sense in further delay.' As Cartwright said this, he picked up a letter opener from his desk and looked ruefully at his companion. 'We may need this.' The other man said nothing, he merely nodded. He looked blankly at his hands.

***

Neither man spoke during the short walk through the woods. Had it not been for their errand it would have been a pleasant morning. The sunlight twinkled on the white-coated grass, and the sharp scent of frost permeated the air. Worthington observed silently that it would not be long before the winter snows settled on the little town. Cartwright slowed up.

'It is just through here.' He stepped from the path and led Worthington between a cluster of trees and into a large clearing.

'What now?'

'I'm not sure. I am certain that this is the spot, and yet I cannot account for the lake.' The cut on Worthington's hand began to throb. He turned suddenly, startled by a noise behind him; a rook taking off, nothing more. He turned back to Cartwright.

'Perhaps we need to recreate your dream, as nearly as possible.' He looked at his hand and sighed. 'Hand me the knife.' Cartwright looked at him for a moment but handed over the knife without objection.

Worthington took the knife firmly in his right hand, and steadying himself with a deep breath, pressed the sharp edge of the blade firmly into his injured left. Blood began to well up in his palm; he tilted his hand so that the blood dripped downwards and mingled with the frost on the cold earth below.

As the first drop hit the ground, he was conscious of a rumbling sensation beneath his feet. He stumbled back. Within seconds the ground was shaking so violently that he could barely keep to his feet. Cartwright cried out in alarm and snatched his friend away from the spot just in time to see the ground open up, exactly on the spot where the blood had fallen. The two men backed away towards the trees as the rupture in the earth swelled, covering half the clearing. As they gazed on in dumbstruck horror, they saw the canyon before them fill with water; it shone in vibrant shades of blue and green and rippled with hints of silver in the early morning sunlight. Neither man spoke.

Worthington reached into his old Gladstone bag, where he had stowed the box. Holding the instrument of mischief aloft he felt its protesting shudders and heard the violent hissing sounds from within; he knew what he must do. Cartwright could only stare as Worthington strode towards the newly formed lake.

With an immense swing of his arm, Worthington threw the box in a high arc into the very heart of the lake. It landed with a loud splash and sank without trace below the surface of the water. For a moment all was silent; not even the song of a bird broke the stillness of the clearing. Then, there rose from the lake a fearful noise, which can neither be described nor comprehended. The water turned from tranquil blue to a hideous crimson in an instant and thence to black.

They had barely time to take in the scene before the water returned to its previous hue and peace returned to the clearing. The calm water of the lake betrayed no hint of what had passed. Perhaps it was a trick of the mind, but Cartwright thought for a moment that he had seen a woman, dressed in a long green cloak, at the far side of the lake, smiling at them; but the next moment the image was gone.

Worthington looked down at his hand, which no longer stung him; there was not a mark or cut upon it. The skin was unbroken, and the pain had gone from it. They knew then that they were free. Whatever evil had tried to exert its influence, it was gone now.

To this day neither man can tell you what the meaning of it all was or why the late Nathaniel Cartwright had not left directions for the box's destruction; they have lived in untroubled ignorance ever since.

As for the lake, it still remains if you should wish to see it. The locals say it has magical properties and that it formed in a place which at one time was considered sacred in some way. As is so often the case with these folk tales, the origins and precise details have been lost down the generations. Yet no one passes that place now without a greeting or offering to the kindly spirits who dwell there.

The Haunted Chamber

'Have you ever stayed in a haunted house?' That was the question posed to Mr John Williams at a dinner party a week prior to the peculiar events of this narrative. The faces around the table had looked at him expectantly.

'I have not; nor do I believe that anyone else has,' said he firmly.

'Why, whatever do you mean?' asked a lady by the name of Mrs Mayhew.

'I mean, madam, that there are no such things as haunted houses.'

'What!' cried her husband. 'You don't mean to say that you don't believe?'

'That is precisely what I do mean, my good sir.'

'Good heavens,' said the lady. 'Well, in that case, I shall ask you this, have you ever stayed in a house which is commonly held to be haunted or troubled?' He thought for a moment before answering.

'No, I don't believe so; not to the best of my knowledge anyhow.'

'And yet, you possess certainty enough to declare the whole thing a humbug?' asked Mr Mayhew in bemusement.

'I do, sir. I am a rational man, and I find the concept of the supernatural to be incongruous with rational thought.'

'Well, you may call me irrational if you wish, Mr Williams,' put in Mrs Mayhew. 'We women are used to being branded as such, most unfairly I might add, but I for one hold that the supernatural does exist.'

'As do I,' announced another of the company, a lady by the name of Mrs Hopkins.

'It seems you're outnumbered, old chap,' laughed Mayhew. At that point, Mr Hopkins, who had been listening in silent amusement all this time, spoke up.

'What if I were to tell you,' said he leaning in, 'that you have in fact spent more than one night in a haunted house?' All eyes turned to him.

'Whatever do you mean?' asked Williams in bewilderment.

'Well, you have been a guest in my home on many occasions, have you not?'

'Do you mean to say that your house is haunted?' asked Mrs Mayhew in wonder.

'I do.'

'Oh! How thrilling,' said she, clapping her hands together gleefully.

'What is this? I have never heard anything of the sort,' blustered Williams.

'George doesn't usually like to tell guests, for fear of making them nervous,' said Mrs Hopkins.

'If I lived in a haunted house I should tell everyone!' declared Mrs Mayhew enthusiastically. Hopkins laughed.

'Well, perhaps it is not strictly true to say that the house is haunted, rather it is just one bedroom,' said he.

'Oh, but this is excellent,' cried Mrs Mayhew. 'Why not conduct an experiment by having Mr Williams spend the night in the haunted chamber?'

'Capital!' declared her husband. 'Come, sir,' said he, his mouth twitching with thinly concealed mirth, 'surely a man of rational and logical mind, such as yourself, must welcome an experiment in the spirit of inquiry.' Williams thought that he put a little more emphasis than was strictly necessary on the word "*spirit*", but he took it in good part. 'A chance to prove us all wrong,' continued Mayhew. 'What objection could there be?'

'Certainly, certainly.' Williams nodded. 'I have no objection; I am always prepared to back my opinions.'

'I do not think Mr Williams would care for the room,' said Mrs Hopkins with a wry smile.

'True enough,' laughed Hopkins. 'But if he will take his chances I've no objection.'

And that is how the same party came to reassemble a week later in the home of Mr and Mrs Hopkins. The activities of the day were uneventful and may be safely passed over. When the night drew in and the hour for bed approached the talk naturally turned again to the haunted chamber.

'Now, Williams,' said Hopkins, 'I have told you nothing of the nature of the disturbance in your room, nor will I; that way if you should experience anything you cannot say that I planted the idea.'

'That is perfectly reasonable,' said Williams.

'Oh, Mr Williams, aren't you at all nervous?' asked Mrs Mayhew.

'Not in the least, madam,' said he with a hint of disapproval. 'These notions of ghosts and hauntings are all a matter of imagination and suggestion. I do myself no disservice when I say that I have never been credited as a man of much imagination, nor do I consider myself to be very easily suggestible.' This was no more than the unadulterated truth; indeed, not even the most generous of Williams's friends would describe him as open-minded. There was only one correct way of viewing the world, and it was his way.

Thus it was that the party, having bid each other goodnight, were despatched forth to their separate quarters and Williams to his haunted chamber. He treated the matter with great unconcern. He would be proved right, no doubt, and being seen to be right was one of his keenest pleasures in life.

Upon first entering his lodging earlier in the day, it had struck him at once what a shame it was that so fine a chamber should have been so long neglected. The room was spacious enough, though a large four-poster bed took up a fair amount of floor space. An old press stood in one corner, a washstand close beside it, and there was a small table positioned by the bed. The walls were lined with fine, old oak panelling which, with the stone mullions of the windows, gave a pleasant appearance of dignified age. Whatever the cause of the room's troubled reputation it was not likely to bother him. Yes, he would be very comfortable here.

In a very short time, he was fast asleep and snoring mightily. He awoke again as the last chimes of midnight were dying away, and he was conscious of a cold draught stirring about the bedclothes. *Strange*, there was no window open in the room when he went to sleep; where then was the draught coming from? Forcing his eyelids open he looked lazily about him and then allowed them to fall closed again. There was the briefest of pauses after which his eyes sprang open again; he was far more alert this time.

To his wonderment, he found he was in the middle of a large, moonlit lawn, with the starry night sky looking down on him. He might understandably have believed that he had suffered an attack of somnambulism if it had not been for the fact that he was still in the four-poster bed.

Not being, as has already been established, a man of great imagination, he could not credit the idea that he had, whilst sleepwalking, single-handedly removed a four poster bed from his room, in its entirety, brought it down two flights of stairs and deposited it on the main lawn; it simply wasn't logical.

He suspected his friends of playing a prank on him; though how they could have managed it was beyond comprehension. Well, he was not going to be so easily rattled as that. He would, forthwith, march straight back to his room and see what he found.

He climbed out of the bed, shivering as his feet touched the damp grass. He made his way quickly across the lawn to the front door, his nightshirt flapping in the blustery autumn wind. The door was not locked. This heightened his suspicions that some plot was afoot to make a fool of him. He was irritated.

He stormed back up the two flights of stairs and along the corridor, feeling his way along the walls until he was back at the door of his own room. He burst into the room and, feeling for the matches, he lighted a candle and looked about him. He saw that the bed was indeed missing. Well, he wasn't about to spend the night out of doors, bed or no bed! No, he had agreed to spend the night in the room, and that's just what he intended to do.

He found some blankets in the press and, blowing out the candle, settled himself down on the floor and attempted to go back to sleep; Mr Williams was prone to stubbornness.

He was almost asleep again when he heard a scratching sound coming from the door. He was in a very ill temper. He was still convinced that the others were trying to play tricks on him, to convince him of the existence of the supernatural. He determined to catch them at it. He rose from the floor and tiptoed silently to the door. The scratching sound continued. Smiling to himself he swung the door back, expecting to see one or more of the company looking shamefaced outside the door. What he saw was in fact much stranger; he saw no one. He frowned, puzzled. They hadn't had time to get away; *they must be hiding somewhere.* He determined to investigate.

He relit the candle and stepped out into the corridor. As soon as his feet were over the threshold the door slammed shut behind him. *A draught no doubt.* Yet the candle had not gone out. He did not concern himself with the door for the present but confined himself to the examination of the corridor.

Having peered into corners and behind tapestries and found no alcoves he turned his attention to the walls. He expected to find some sort of passageway or bolthole, which was not uncommon in old houses. After a close examination of the panelling revealed nothing, he was feeling vexed. He stomped off back to his room and tried the door only to find that it was stuck fast. He was growing increasingly impatient; if these were pranks then they were in very poor taste. He put down his candle and tried to force the door open; it would not yield. In frustration he threw himself at the door; it burst open suddenly, depositing him in a very undignified heap upon the floor. He stood up, brushed himself off and looked about him angrily. Aided by the moonlight, he saw to his great surprise that he was not in the room he had just left. He blinked. Surely he could not have made an error and entered the wrong room?

He stepped back into the corridor, picked up his candle, and was immensely confused to find that it was not the same corridor he had just entered from. For the first time, his conviction was beginning to waver. He looked out of a window and, by the light of the moon, could make out just enough of the scene below to tell him, to his utter bewilderment, that he was now on the opposite side of the house! *How could such a thing be?*

He was beginning to panic. He was no longer sure of himself, and he was a man who was always sure of himself; this new-found uncertainty did not sit well with him. Tracing his way carefully through the house, he worked his way back to his own room. He pushed the door open and sprang back, a precaution against any tricks that might be awaiting him. Edging forwards reluctantly he peered into the room. He saw nothing untoward, barring the absence of the bed. Finally, his pride overcame his reluctance and he shuffled into the room. As he reached the centre of the terrible chamber the door swung shut behind him, closing him inside.

***

The following morning when the maid took Mr Williams his tea she received no answer to her knocking. She called out, but there was no response. Leaving the tea tray on the table outside the door, she went off to inform her mistress;

'Oh dear,' said Mrs Hopkins to her husband. 'I do hope poor Mr Williams hasn't had too uncomfortable a night.'

'Nonsense, my dear. A bit of a fright will do him good. I expect after last night he won't be so quick to deny the existence of the supernatural,' he laughed. 'Don't you worry,' said he kissing his wife tenderly on the head. 'I shall go and make sure he's all right.'

Imagine then his surprise when he found the room empty. The bed was back in its usual place, but there was no sign of the occupant, yet his possessions remained. *Odd* he thought. *I wonder.*

He questioned the servants who confirmed that the doors were still shut up tight when they had woken, and no one had left the house since.

They discussed the matter over breakfast. Mrs Mayhew was of the opinion that he had run off rather than face them with the admission that they had been right all along, but she could offer no explanations for the locked doors or as to why he would leave his things behind in his flight. Hopkins had his own ideas. They did not have long to wait, however, for news of Williams.

A telegram arrived during breakfast; it was from the man himself. It read as follows,

"Most damnable room I ever slept in. Woke up in bed at The Willows. No idea how. Regret cannot make breakfast."

The Willows was Mr Williams's country residence, which lay at some twenty miles distance from that of Hopkins. No amount of rational thought on their part could explain how Mr Williams, without his knowledge, could have travelled twenty miles, in the middle of a bitter autumn night, clad only in a nightshirt and with nothing upon his feet.

As for Williams, if you were to ask him now whether he believed in the supernatural you might get a very different answer.

The Inn by the Crossroads

There is a village by the name of Meddleford, which sprang up at the meeting point of two major roads. There was once an inn situated there, overlooking the crossroads. In all the time I knew it, it had always stood empty, abandoned and forlorn. Though it must once have been a pretty little dwelling, it was by then beginning to show signs of its age and neglect, an ivy-covered and crumbling ruin.

It had an evil name amongst the locals. The last landlord there, it is said, was an unsavoury type who kept all sorts of undesirable company.

Nothing would induce the villagers to pass the inn after dusk. To avoid the crossroads often meant a considerable diversion, often over open countryside, yet this was considered preferable by many when necessity compelled them to venture out in the evening.

There is another inn on the far side of the village, which if less conveniently situated for travellers is at least more agreeable to local tastes. It is in the bar of this inn that the men of the town stop to quench their thirst of an evening.

One such evening, when I was still quite new to the village, I inquired of the landlord about the other establishment's reputation and the custom of avoiding the place after dark.

'Well, sir,' said he, 'the last landlord disappeared there some twenty years past. He was a bad sort, a drunkard with a bad temper when he had a drop inside him and none too friendly when he was sober; yet his wife was the sweetest and fairest creature you would ever hope to meet. It was a regular wonder hereabouts how such a woman could permit herself to be tied to such a roaring tyrant as he, or that her parents would consent to such a marriage for that matter. A miserable life he gave her, and perhaps it was a mercy when she died just two years later.

'Well, that's when the rumours started. It was said that one night, on that very crossroads, he met the devil himself and they made a pact together. He sold his soul that he might have the girl.

'Then, not long before they became engaged, his bitter rival, and the girls favourite, was found dead upon the crossroads; naturally, he was suspected, but nothing could ever be proved against him and the cause of death was a mystery. There was not a mark upon the body, and he had been in the best of health. There was nothing to go on but the look of horror etched into the features of the corpse. There the matter lay for a time.

'Then one day, he disappears in the night. There were those who claimed they saw him being dragged off bodily, but it was a foggy night and they could swear to nothing definite. There are some who say he was carried off by the devil or his agents, come to claim him.

'Ever since then folks have avoided the place as much as possible, especially after dark. If you ask me there are others have the use of it now.' When I asked him what he meant by this last statement he declined to elaborate.

Naturally, I found this to be a very curious piece of local folklore, but that was all it was to me. Yet there was certainly a decided air of desolation about the place, which I have often found to be the case with abandoned buildings.

I did not give very much more thought to the abandoned inn until one winter evening late in October, All Hallows' Eve to be precise, when a stranger came to the bar. For the first scene of my story, I must rely on the reports of others, for I was not present at the outset.

This stranger, we shall call him Sanford, had arranged to meet a friend there, and they were to travel on together the following day. His friend, whom we shall call Chambers, was engaged in conversation with some of the locals when Sanford arrived; he called him over.

'You are late, Sanford; I expected you an hour ago.'

'Yes, I was detained in town,' said he, 'then I almost went to the wrong inn; you never told me there were two inns in the village. It might have saved some bother if we had arranged to meet at the inn by the crossroads.'

'Ah, but if you passed it then you must surely have noticed that it is untenanted,' said his friend, who was well acquainted with the village and knew the reputation of the inn.

'Don't be absurd; I passed there not twenty minutes ago and the lights were on within.' The other men at the table frowned.

'But that is very odd; nobody has set foot in that place for twenty years from what I gather.' There were nods of agreement from their fellow drinkers.

'Well, it is occupied now at any rate.' His friend fell silent.

As the evening progressed and the drinks flowed Chambers returned to the subject of the inn. This time he drew the landlord, who was not averse to sharing his story with the stranger, into the conversation.

'But you don't mean to say that you came via the crossroads tonight, sir? inquired the landlord.

'Well of course I did; it is the quickest and most direct route into the village.' An old man in the corner made the sign of the cross. Sanford did not notice, or if he did he chose not to acknowledge it.

'And you saw lights on at the inn?' By now a hush had fallen over the little bar room, and all eyes were turned on the stranger. He shifted uncomfortably under their collective scrutiny.

'Yes, there were lights on. What of it?'

'And people, were there people?' asked the landlord ignoring the question.

'Yes, there were people,' said Sanford irritably. 'I tell you the inn is occupied. I've had enough of this nonsense. I shall go there and partake of a glass, if only to prove to you all that these phantoms are nothing but imagination. I may have a more lively evening of it.' Emboldened by drink, he staggered out into the night, despite the protestations of his friend and the others. Yet no one went after him; their fear held them fast.

'He may well have a more lively night,' remarked the landlord. 'Whatever company is gathered in that place, tonight of all nights, is not one I should care to know.' The bar room fell into silence. The previously cheerful atmosphere became subdued and tense.

Half an hour passed and Sanford did not return, nor did anyone move to leave. There was a sense of expectation in the air.

Suddenly, a cold draught blew through the little bar room; everyone looked up, alert. The door had opened and in the doorway stood the old priest, Father O'Kelly.

'Good evening to you, Joe,' said he to the landlord.

'Good evening, Father; what can I get you?'

'A drop of your brandy would be most welcome, Joe. I've been out visiting one of my flock, who has taken ill, and it's no night for a man of my years to be aboard. The cold gets into my old bones something awful.' He sipped the proffered brandy appreciatively; looking about him, he saw for the first time the downcast eyes and heard the overwhelming silence of his fellow drinkers.

'What's this now?' said he. 'Why, there's a shocking gloom about you all tonight. What's dampened your spirits so?' Someone flinched at his words. They told him briefly what had occurred, and he stared at them, open-mouthed.

'You don't mean to say you let the poor soul venture alone into that den of devils and not a man of you lifted a finger to stop him?' They all looked guiltily at one another. The landlord coloured deeply as he said,

'We were afraid, Father.'

'Well, I cannot blame you for that, but something must be done if it is not already too late. I must go after him.' Chambers spoke in horrified tones,

'You can't go there alone, Father!'

97

'Then you shall come with me.' Chambers said nothing, not wanting to appear a coward next to the elderly priest.

'We should all go,' said the landlord. All eyes turned to him.

'It'll be safer if we all go; besides, what would dare to harm us when we have a man of God with us?' A murmur went around the bar room, and soon everyone was on their feet and preparing to leave. Lanterns were fetched and such weapons as could be mustered, and the party bustled out into the night. Father O'Kelly led the lantern-lit procession through the village towards the crossroads. The men fell into silent step behind him.

I met the party in the street coming the opposite way. On hearing of their errand, I joined myself willingly to their number. People appeared at doors and windows, peering curiously at the strange party. Some shouted out to know what the matter was; on catching the brief replies that were thrown back some hurried to join us.

The night was bitter, and a sharp wind wound around our ankles as we hurried through the night. The frosty air was biting at our flesh, the cold seeping beneath our skin and chilling us to the bone.

By the time we reached the crossroads, we could barely see the road for the shroud of frozen fog that lay thick and heavy before us; our own white breath swirled and mingled with it. Holding the lanterns before us, we proceeded cautiously in the direction of the inn.

The priest held up a hand to silence the murmurs of the crowd and signalled for us to listen. As silence fell over the party, the sound of music could be heard drifting on the fog.

'It's coming from the inn,' whispered the priest.

'Then it's true; there is… something there,' said Joe. A mummer of unrest rippled through our number. The priest took from around his neck a crucifix, which he handed to Joe.

'Hold it tightly before you and do not waver; have faith.' He said no more. Joe nodded and took it without a word.

Then the priest reached into his pocket and removed a small bottle of holy water, which he grasped in his trembling hand.

As we moved forward, we could dimly see the lights of the inn through the fog. There came the sound of laughter from within, but it inspired no feelings of joy in those who heard it. Our blood ran cold at the sound.

Just as we were trying to decide how to proceed, we discerned a group of figures coming from the inn. Chambers almost cried out when he saw that one of the figures was Sanford, but the sound died in his throat as he saw that he was not walking from the inn but being dragged roughly by his two companions. How am I to communicate their appearance to you? I find I positively shrink from the recollection. If I were to describe it as that of smoke and shadow made flesh, insubstantial, incorporeal, you might have some idea, though very little; the only thing I am certain of is that, whatever else they were, they were not human.

Sanford struggled and fought fiercely to get away as the others drove him on towards the crossroads, but their strength was greater.

'Why struggle so?' said one of his captors. 'You were glad enough of our company not so long ago.'

'The likes of you are as brethren to us,' said the other. The rescuers gaped in silent horror. Finding his voice, at last, the priest shouted,

'Now!' The rescue party fell upon Sanford's captors, some swinging wildly with their sticks, some throwing stones. Joe, holding the priest's cross before him, drove them back. One hissed in diabolical rage as Father O'Kelly showered him with the holy water; the hiss grew into a howl, and to our absolute horror the ground began to shake violently beneath us. Suddenly, in a flash of searing heat, two great columns of fire sprang forth from the ground and joined together to form a monstrous archway of flame.

Blinded by the sudden heat and the dense fog, we fell back, but it was too late for Sanford's captors; as they made a last futile attempt to drag him through the fire with them, the priest came at them again as Joe fought to pull Sanford free of their trap. With a cry of rage, they let go of their victim and dived through the fiery archway, which vanished as quickly as it had appeared.

Sanford and Joe had toppled over and lay in a heap on the frozen earth. Sanford's face was a mask of sheer horror and terror. He was taken back to the safety of the other inn and was tended carefully by the doctor; even so, it was several weeks before he could sleep through a whole night and not be awoken by nightmares.

A few nights after these events, an unexplained fire broke out at the old inn on the crossroads, which razed it to the ground.

Yet, there are those who say that sometimes, on a foggy night, you can still see the old inn and hear the strange and terrible music that issues from it; but don't linger too long, in case you should meet the revellers at the crossroads.

Sir Henry's Folly

There is a hill known locally as Maiden's Hill, and it is there that Sir Henry Morstan stood, gazing out and down at his grounds and the wide expanse of open countryside surrounding them.

'The builders should be here very shortly to begin the work, Sir Henry,' Mr Forbes his steward was saying to him.

'Very good, Forbes.' He smiled contentedly. 'It is an excellent spot is it not?'

'Oh undoubtedly, sir. One of the finest views on the whole estate to my thinking, sir.'

It was true; Maiden's Hill was the highest point on the estate; from there, on a clear day, the view was unsurpassed. Now it was to be the site of Sir Henry's new folly, a tower twenty feet high looking out for miles in every direction. It would give the place, Sir Henry reflected, quite a romantic air.

The builders arrived in the course of the morning with their materials, and work commenced. Here we may safely leave them until the morrow.

The following day being clear and cloudless, though perhaps a little chilly, Sir Henry decided that he would take a walk after breakfast and perhaps go by way of Maiden's Hill.

The sun shone brightly overhead, and the cool spring breezes stirred around the ends of his coat. Maiden's Hill reared before him, dominating the landscape. He congratulated himself inwardly on his choice of location.

He wound his way slowly up the well-trodden path to the summit. He had expected to see the builders going busily about their labours; instead, to his great surprise, he found them standing about in bewildered formation.

Mr Brooks, the foreman, was engaged in animated conversation with Mr Forbes. The little man was positively crimson and shaking his fist in the air in a most undignified manner.

'Whatever is going on here?' cried Sir Henry. Startled by his unperceived arrival the two men immediately straightened up and looked awkwardly at one another.

'It seems, sir,' said Forbes, 'that there has been some mischief here during the night.'

'Mischief? What sort of mischief?' asked Sir Henry.

'All the materials, Sir Henry, someone has made off with them!' cried Mr Brooks. 'How am I to build without materials I should like to know? And am I to be held responsible if this here building, not that there is a building yet, is not completed as soon as you might have desired, sir?' Sir Henry frowned.

'That is very vexing, to be sure,' said he, 'but I shall see that you are properly recompensed for any losses Mr Brooks. The materials were taken from my land, and I must bear the responsibility.' At this, the crimson of Mr Brooks's face came down several shades to its more customary hue of ruddy pink.

'Well that's very decent of you, Sir Henry, I'm sure, to take it so well.'

'Not at all; not at all. Now, Forbes.'

'Yes, Sir Henry?' said Mr Forbes, evidently relieved by the end of Mr Brooks's lengthy tirade.

'I want you to look into this matter, and see that Mr Brooks is taken care of.'

'Very good, sir.'

Sir Henry left them to their business and he, in turn, went about his, albeit in a much less agreeable mood than he had started out in.

An hour later Mr Forbes found him in his study.

'Well?' he asked.

'We found the materials all right, sir.'

'Excellent! Where were they?'

'On the hill overlooking the lake, sir.'

'How very peculiar. Why on earth would anyone do such a thing?'

'I can't imagine, sir. Probably just some local lads up to a bit of mischief, sir.'

'Yes, I dare say; yet it seems rather far for them to cart the things just for a bit of fun at old Brooks's expense.'

'Well, I've made arrangements to have the things taken back anyhow, sir.'

'Very good, Forbes.'

'Sir Henry.' And with that Mr Forbes withdrew.

Sir Henry's ill humour had lifted, but he was at a loss to understand why anyone would play such a trick. Still, he thought, it was all right now.

But that was not to be the last Sir Henry heard of the matter, for the following morning saw the incident repeated and again the next. Mr Brooks was fit to be tied, and Sir Henry was not very much happier himself.

On the fourth evening, he decided that he would take a stroll up to the spot and see if he could catch sight of the miscreants. Mr Forbes had been watching the hill but always managed to arrive after the deed was done.

Only after he had reached the foot of the hill did it occur to Sir Henry that perhaps he might have been wiser to bring one or two men with him or at least tell Forbes where he was going. Supposing he surprised the culprits in the act and they took alarm and set about him.

He did not turn back, however. As he approached he thought he saw, in the half-light, a figure moving on the hillside. Steeling himself, he crept slowly forwards. To his surprise, it was not a ruffian whom he came face to face with.

A young woman, clad in a long dress of green wool with a cord of silver tied about her waist, was sat on the hillside. She held in her hand a silver comb with which she was combing the abundant waves of auburn hair that flowed down over her shoulders and came to rest at her waist.

So captivated was he that he stood in silent awe, mesmerised by the gentle, repetitive, gliding motion of the comb. He thought that he had never seen such beauty as this before and never would again if he should live to be a hundred.

She raised her eyes to his, and his heart leapt as she smiled sweetly upon him.

'Good evening to you, sir,' said she.

'Good evening, miss,' said he removing his hat. 'And who might you be? I don't believe we have met.' If they had met before he was hardly likely to forget it.

'There are those who once called me The Maiden of the Hill, but those days are long gone.' She smiled sadly, her eyes downcast.

Maiden's Hill? Surely not. Sir Henry pushed the unbidden thought away.

'What sort of answer is that?' he asked a little impatiently.

'It will do for now.' She smiled her disarming smile again and all his ill temper melted away once more. His senses reeled. Recalling himself for a moment, he realised that the materials were gone again.

'The building materials are gone!' Did you see anyone move them?'

'Aye.'

'Who was it? Quick tell me; where did they go, towards the lake? When?' he asked hurriedly. She clicked her tongue in mock annoyance.

'So many questions! It was I who moved them.'

'You?' he asked in astonishment. He could hardly see this delicate girl carrying heavy building materials over hill and dale. 'How did you move them?'

'It matters not.'

'Matters not? Well, it matters a good deal to me, my girl.' One of the girl's eyebrows arched slightly. Her lips curved into an amused little smile.

'Oh, come now; don't be cross with me,' said she teasingly. She held him in her gaze, and he was overcome with the feeling that to be angry with such a creature as she would be a sin indeed. Her beauty was intoxicating.

'But why?' he managed at last.

'Because you cannot build here.'

'Why ever not?'

'Because I live here; that's why.'

'You? Live here? But it's just a bare hill. I own this land and I think I would know if anyone were living on it.'

'Is that so?'

'It is.'

'Do you mean to say that you don't believe in anything that your eyes cannot see?'

'Of course.'

'Well, how absurd.'

'Oh, and why do you say it is absurd?'

'You cannot see the air around you, yet you must depend on it for your survival. There are many things in this world that go unseen by mortal men.'

'You bewilder me,' he sighed in exasperation. She nodded complacently, as though this were only to be expected.

'Well,' said she, 'if it is proof you require then I suppose you must have it.' As she spoke her blue eyes sparkled with a silver sheen, as of moonlight.

To his amazement, he observed that a heavy looking oaken door was set into the side of the great hill. His eyes took a moment to adjust.

'It is rather chilly tonight,' she continued. 'Perhaps you would be more comfortable if we continued our talk indoors. Would you care to step inside?'

Sir Henry was not at all sure that he would care to, nor was he certain about the propriety of acceding to such a request. However, he followed mutely as the maiden pushed the door open and led him inside.

He found himself in a large round room, the walls of which seemed to be lined with something resembling daub. In the middle of the room a fire was burning, its thin grey smoke rolling up and out through a hole in the centre of the thatched roof; this rather led him to wonder where the smoke went if they were inside the hill. He may have raised the question if he had not been distracted at that moment by the sudden realisation that the door through which they had entered had disappeared; not a trace of it remained, and the wall seemed wholly undisturbed, as though no door had ever been. There was, however, a door on the other side of the hut, which gave him some measure of reassurance, though admittedly very little.

'Perhaps you would care for a little refreshment?' She crossed the room and took up a silver jug from a small wooden table and poured the contents into two silver goblets. She handed one of the goblets to him. He looked at the vessel uncertainly. She seemed amused.

'Do not worry,' said she. 'It is perfectly safe. You may exchange it for mine if you prefer.'

'No, no that's quite all right' said Sir Henry, but still he did not drink. Watching him closely she raised her own drink to her lips, then turned and beckoned him towards the fire.

'Come, join me.' She sat cross-legged before the fire, her pale features illuminated softly in the glow of the firelight. As he sat opposite her, staring into the shifting flames, she leaned towards him suddenly.

'Do you fear me?' she whispered. Did he fear her? Could he even be sure she was real? He feared for his sanity.

'No,' he replied after a moment's hesitation. 'No, I mean, that is...'

'You do!' He was not entirely sure whether her tone was one of triumph or disappointment. He decided it seemed closer to the latter.

'You need not fear me, Sir Henry.' He wondered how she knew his name but decided he probably would not care for the answer, so forbore to ask.

Her eyes settled on his goblet. *Such remarkably pretty eyes.* He drank deep. The sweet liquid slid softly down his throat; he felt its gentle warmth spreading through him, as though bringing warmth to his very soul. The gesture seemed to please her.

'There, you see; that wasn't so bad now was it?' She gave a pleasant little laugh, which conjured in his mind a curious image of silver bells tinkling in the breeze. He could not keep from smiling at this bewitching stranger. Moving closer to him, she said,

'Now, let us discuss your folly.'

***

The following day Mr Brooks received his orders, and arrangements were made for the relocation of the folly. It was now to be built on the hill overlooking the lake.

Time passed, and Sir Henry's folly was built without further mishap. Its new location, if not quite so high as Maiden's Hill, did at least have views which were equally pleasant. In fact, Sir Henry found that, after all, he preferred the new location.

Some said Sir Henry was foolish to move his entire project because of a silly joke, though no culprit was ever named. Others would smile knowingly when the subject was raised. Some called the tower Sir Henry's Folly and some The Maiden's Tower, in honour of its original location or perhaps for reasons of their own.

Sir Henry would often stroll up to the top of the tower on a clear evening and look out over the lake. Sometimes he took friends to the spot to show them the very admirable view.

And when he married, it was there that he took his new bride that she might see, to best advantage, her new home. Standing atop of the tower she closed her eyes and smiled serenely as a soft breeze caught at her auburn hair.

The Crying Ghost

It was spring when she had first come to Lastford. The trees overhead had already begun forming themselves into a lush green canopy and the flowers in the garden of the lodge had been showing signs of their first buds. The whole world had seemed to vibrate then with the promise of new life. She had watched her new husband, Neville, as he'd exchange greetings with the lodge-keeper. Her husband, so handsome, with those dark eyes and that strong jaw. He had smiled at her and she had blushed beneath his gaze, his shy young bride. The heavy iron gates had swung back and her new life had opened up before her.

Two years had passed since then, and Jane had settled into her role as mistress of Lastford. On the whole, they were still as happy and content with each other as they had been on that first day. There was but one thing that they desired to make their happiness complete, a child, an heir to the family seat. She knew what it meant to her husband. So, every night Jane went to sleep with a silent prayer upon her lips that they might be so blessed.

One such night, she lay restless, the night being too hot and oppressive to allow of anything but the lightest sleep. Finally, tiredness won out and she fell into a fitful doze.

No sooner had she drifted off, however, than she was startled awake again. Drowsy and confused she could not for the moment recall what had awakened her, but as her senses returned to her she remembered. She had heard something, the unmistakable sound of a woman crying. Surely not. Who could it have been? Not one of the servants, for their rooms were in a separate part of the house. Even with the windows open to the night air, she could not expect to hear any sound so clearly from that quarter. No, the sound had been nearer than that.

She glanced over to where the pale moonlight fell on the still sleeping figure in the bed beside her. He did not stir. It must, she decided, have been a dream otherwise he would surely have woken also, for he was a light sleeper as a rule. She dismissed the matter and closed her eyes again, and so she slept; but she was not easy, for she dreamed with a strange clarity; a dream which she recounted to her husband over breakfast.

'You look a little tired today, my dear; did you not sleep well?' he asked.

'No, indeed not. I'm afraid it was a little hot last night, and it kept me awake until quite late.'

'Yes, it was rather warm.'

'I'm afraid the heat must have upset me rather, for just as I was falling asleep I was sure I heard a woman crying; I heard it most distinctly, and it woke me up again. Then when I went back to sleep I dreamt of it again, but this time I did not wake.

'The sound persisted, and I remember thinking, whoever she is, she must have great sorrows, for she was crying as though her heart must break from it. I listened until I could stand it no longer; then I arose and made my way from the room. I really felt I had to find her, that she needed me somehow. I traced the sound to the empty room opposite our own. I opened the door slowly and crept inside. There was a woman standing by the window, with her back to me. She was sobbing uncontrollably. I moved towards her, intending to try to comfort her, but that is when I awoke.'

'Indeed, that is very curious,' said her husband. 'Probably the heat, as you say. Well, I hope you have a better night tonight, my dear.' He said no more, though she rather fancied there was something on his mind.

But this was not to be the end of the matter, for the figure of the crying woman was to become a regular feature of her dreams. Her husband wanted to call in a doctor, but she put him off; she felt a curious aversion to the idea, and she did not actually feel as though she were unwell. Apart from the curious dreams, the familiar rhythms of life, on the whole, continued undisturbed.

One morning, the weather being so fine, she thought it a pity to waste the day indoors; so, she decided to take her book outside and enjoy the sunshine for an hour or so. She asked the maid to bring out some lemonade to her on the lawn, and she sat herself down at the little garden table with her parasol and book. The day was warm and the gentle summer breezes lulled her. She sat back in her chair, closing her eyes and listening to the birdsong and the soft hum of a nearby bumblebee. It was a glorious summer day.

It was then that it happened, that slow, creeping certainty that one is being watched. She opened her eyes, half expecting to see the maid, but she was alone, the serenity of the garden undisturbed.

She felt her eyes being drawn irresistibly upwards to one of the first-floor windows, the very window which had featured so often in her dreams. There framed against the casement she saw a young woman looking down at her. She started, her eyes fixed on the figure. The summer seemed to melt away, and she shivered. She was aware only of herself and the figure. She jumped again as a voice beside her spoke, and the world rushed back in.

'Your lemonade, madam.' It was the maid. She stared at the girl and then back to the window; the figure was gone.

'Saunders, has someone been upstairs just now?' The maid looked surprised.

'No, madam.'

'How odd; I was sure I saw someone in one of the upstairs windows.' She laughed as lightly as she was able. 'I must have been deceived. A shadow no doubt.'

The next few days saw no return of either the dream or her visitant, and she began to hope that whatever had caused it all had passed. In truth, she was beginning to wonder if her experiences were the result of some disturbance of the mind after all.

It was perhaps a week later that she was seated alone in her parlour. It had been raining most of the morning so that she was obliged to pass her time indoors. She sat with her needlework on her lap, but her eyes continually strayed to the window, following the path of the occasional raindrop as it meandered down the glass. She found her mind turning once again to her strange visitant. Had she really been a mere delusion, or could the house be haunted? But the idea was absurd; if the house were haunted why should she only now be seeing the ghost for the first time, after two years in the place? It made no sense. There was something else that did not make sense; something that, in her first shock, had not occurred to her at the time, though the thought was beginning to take shape now with alarming clarity.

A sudden and dreadful commotion brought her back to herself. It came from the hall, a terrible crashing, someone falling down the stairs! The sound came to a stop with a sickening thud. She sprang up in alarm, her needlework falling at her feet. She ran to the door and threw it open expecting to find her maid injured, or worse. But, to her great surprise, there was no one and nothing to account for the noise. She cast her eyes about wildly, looking for an explanation for the disturbance, but she found none. The room began to swim before her. How she kept from crying out she could not have said. Somehow, she found her way back to the parlour.

The afternoon saw the rain stop and the sun begin to emerge. Feeling uneasy in her mind and desiring a little company and advice, she made up her mind to pay a visit to her friend Mrs Morrison, who was a close neighbour.

They took tea together and chatted quite amiably so that after a time she began to feel more herself than she had done for several weeks. She was undecided for a time how to raise the subject that was foremost in her mind. She did not want to be thought of as mad, but she felt that she simply must tell someone. She knew that she could trust her friend to take her fears seriously and to give her sound and reasonable advice. Finally, she plucked up the courage and told her friend in hurried explanations all that was troubling her.

'I know,' said she, 'what Neville will say if I tell him; that it is all fancy, that my senses are disturbed and I should see a doctor. But really you know, I don't feel in the least bit unwell.'

'Do you believe then that what you saw was a ghost?' asked Mrs Morrison with great interest.

'I do not know what to believe. I no longer feel that I can trust my own senses. Perhaps it was a ghost, yet if that is so then it really makes no sense to me.'

'How so?' Jane looked embarrassed and said almost apologetically,

'Because I feel sure that the woman I saw was with child! I ask you, whoever heard of an expectant ghost?' She could not help but laugh at the absurdity of it. 'Perhaps Neville is right; perhaps I am unwell, mad even. I dare say he would call it a delusion and blame it all on my own desire for a child.' She blushed heavily, a little ashamed at her indiscretion. Her friend smiled kindly, and she went on. 'But that cannot explain what happened to me this morning. Oh, Sarah, tell me what does it all mean?'

Her friend had listened with keen interest, and when Jane had finished speaking the other woman's expression was thoughtful.

'Firstly, I do not think you are mad, Jane dear; you may put that thought out of your head at once. It is men's egos that cause them to blame on hysteria anything which they themselves cannot explain or are not sensible of.' She sighed. 'Rather pitiable really,' said she with a mischievous smile. Then, she grew serious again. 'There has been talk, from time to time, of strange sounds in that house going back some years, sounds of crying such as you describe; it is usually women who hear it, but I have never before heard of anyone actually seeing her.'

Ah! So that was why Neville had looked so uncomfortable when she had mentioned her dream; he did not wish to frighten her by telling her the house was haunted. Mrs Morrison rose abruptly.

'Come, I have something I wish to show you,' said she holding out her hand. Jane took it and allowed her friend to lead her where she would.

They passed through the hall and up the stairs. At the top of the stairs, on the wall facing them was a large gilt-framed portrait of a fair-skinned, young woman in Regency dress. There was an audible intake of breath as Jane beheld it.

'You recognise her?' asked Mrs Morrison.

'Why, it is she. The very woman I saw in the window and in my dreams,' she stammered. 'But I do not understand.'

'She is Dorothy Mathews. She was once mistress of Lastford, as you are now, though not for very long, poor dear. She was born in this house. The daughter of one of my husband's ancestors. She left here to marry the master of Lastford, Sir John Mathews. I believe his portrait still hangs in your hall.'

'What happened to her?' asked Jane, a rolling uneasiness taking root in her stomach.

'She died young,' replied her friend softly, 'while she was with child.'

'In childbed?'

'No, it was an accident.'

'What kind of accident?' Her friend looked at her earnestly.

'She fell down the stairs.'

***

Jane stood in the hall of her husband's ancestral home gazing up at the portrait of Sir John Mathews. She thought, in that rugged yet friendly looking countenance, she could discern something of Neville's features. As she was thinking on this, her husband came from the dining room to join her.

'Hello! What are you doing standing about in the hall?' he asked as he came up beside her.

'Oh, I was just looking at Sir John. I think I can see a little family resemblance between you,' she said smiling up at him.

'Can you indeed? Well, I suppose there is something about the jaw. Though of course, he was from another branch of the family.'

'Oh?'

'Yes, when he died the estate passed to his younger brother, my grandfather.'

'He had no children?' she asked casting a sideways glance at him. She thought for a moment that she saw his face redden slightly.

'No, no; his wife died young. He never remarried.' At that moment the maid appeared with the coffee, and they retired to the drawing room, where the conversation passed to other matters.

***

That night she lay awake pondering her tragic predecessor and the terrible grief that she carried after death. She thought too of the unhappy Sir John, who had been robbed, in one cruel moment, of his wife and his child. What was it that this woman wanted? Why was it that Jane was the only one to sense her presence? Then, in the dead of night, when all else was silent, it came again. The sound of crying filled the empty silence that surrounded it.

Quickly, she arose in the darkness, her footstep falling noiselessly on the old floorboards and traced the familiar route to the empty room opposite her own. She pushed the door open gently and slipped inside.

Standing by the window once more was the figure of the woman. Unsure whether she was awake or dreaming, she approached the figure; but she did not wake, as was her wont; instead, she stood motionless as the woman ceased her crying and turned towards her. As her silhouette took shape against the moonlit window Jane could see now that the woman was indeed heavy with child. She looked at Jane and smiled warmly. She came forward. Reaching out, she laid her hand upon Jane's stomach. Jane's skin tingled strangely beneath the ghostly hand. Their eyes met, and both women smiled. At last, she understood what it was that Dorothy Mathews wanted.

***

It was spring when her son was born. He was a strong, healthy lad, an heir for Lastford, and she and Neville were happier than ever. As the boy grew, many people remarked that he had inherited the family features from his father, and some even went so far as to say that he bore a marked resemblance to the tragic Sir John.

Shadows

The entrance of John Grey into Hartingby society elicited much interest in the town, as the arrival of any bachelor of good fortune into a country town may be expected to do.

Ladies with unmarried daughters were at pains to make themselves agreeable to the newcomer. If his fortune recommended him to the parents of the town, his company was, due to his handsome countenance, no less sought after by the young ladies themselves.

Though in fortune and features he may have been considered an eligible prospective husband, his manner was not all that could be desired. For one thing, he never laughed, and on the rare occasions when a smile graced his lips it never reached his eyes, which remained cold and unblinking. It left people with the uncomfortable sensation that they were being studied in some way, like specimens in a laboratory.

These peculiarities of temperament meant that the enthusiasm with which he was initially courted was to some degree suppressed as time went on, but it was by no means abandoned.

One family with whom he was a frequent guest were the Simpsons. One evening when Mr and Mrs Simpson and the two Miss Simpsons, Isabella and Maria, were seated after dinner in their drawing room, the conversation turned towards their neighbour.

'I saw Mr Grey in town today, my dear,' Mr Simpson remarked to his wife. 'He inquired after yourself and the girls.'

'That was very civil of him I'm sure,' replied Mrs Simpson. 'And how did you find him?'

'Very well, my dear. He was telling me of the plans he has for the house. He hinted,' said Mr Simpson with a sly glance towards Isabella, 'that what the place really needs is a woman's touch.' Maria cast a look at her sister and suppressed a giggle. 'I think,' continued Mr Simpson, 'that our Isabella has caught Mr Grey's eye. I should not be at all surprised if there is a proposal before very long!' Isabella's eyes widened in shock.

'Oh, Papa,' cried she. 'You must not jest about such things. The very idea!'

'Jest? Not at all, my dear. I am in earnest.'

'Oh! I pray then that you are mistaken, for I assure you I had not an idea of such a thing, and I could take no pleasure in such an occurrence,' said she in great distress.

'Well, well, my dear. There is no need to take on so. I am not a tyrant; I shall not insist upon your acceptance should the matter arise. But still, you might do worse you know. He has a good fortune, and you might find you come to care for him.'

'Oh no, I never shall! There is something very odd about him. I don't know quite what it is, but he gives me the shivers.' And as though to demonstrate her point she gave a little shudder.

'What nonsense,' replied her father. 'Perhaps he is a little stern in his appearance, but there are worse things to be in life than serious, my dear.' To this, Mrs Simpson chimed in,

'I'm afraid I must agree with Isabella, my dear. I am not at all sure that I should be pleased to have such a son in law, fortune or no fortune.'

'Quite,' said Maria. 'He is very handsome, to be sure, but there is something rather frightful about him all the same.'

'Well, well, it seems I must defer to women's intuition.'

'Oh dear,' said Isabella. 'Now that you have told me this, I really dread to meet Mr Grey again. I think I shall die of embarrassment.'

'I'm afraid you will have to do your best to be civil, for I have invited him to dine with us on Tuesday.'

'Tuesday? Surely you have not forgotten, Papa? That is the evening on which Mr Logan is to dine with us,' said Maria. At mention of this gentleman's name, Isabella became very flushed.

'To be sure, I had,' said her father. 'But it is no matter.' On perceiving Isabella's countenance he laughed heartily. 'Ah ha! Now I see the true reason for your condemnation of poor Mr Grey.' At this, Isabella's face went from pink to deep crimson.

'I do believe Mr Logan also has eyes for Isabella,' said Maria. 'Only fancy, Isabella; two suitors to choose from. If all the eligible gentlemen of our acquaintance are to fall in love with you, I shall die a perfect old maid,' she teased.

'There is no fear of that, sister,' said Isabella with a laugh. 'But really I do wish you had not invited Mr Grey, Papa.'

'Well, there is not much to be done about it now. You will just have to make the best of it, my dear.' And so, poor Isabella was left to contemplate an uncomfortable evening ahead.

***

Tuesday came, and Isabella's discomfort was to some extent lessened by the very courteous attentions paid to her by Mr Logan. But even her happiness in this regard could not wholly dispel the sense of gloom which she felt in the presence of Mr Grey.

It seemed that he too had observed Mr Logan's attentions towards her, and evidently, he resented it. Up until her father's revelation, she had been oblivious to Mr Grey's intentions towards her, preoccupied as she was with thoughts of her other suitor. Now, however, she could not fail to notice the dark looks that he threw towards them. She could feel his resentment hanging in the air, though he was always perfectly civil in his speech.

During the course of the evening, there was something of a contest of wills to engage her in conversation. Though she had no wish to appear discourteous towards Mr Grey, she was always conscious of inadvertently offering anything that might be construed as encouragement. It put her in a most difficult position. Though her mother and sister did their best to distract Mr Grey, his eyes continually returned to Isabella and his rival.

On one occasion Isabella looked up to see Grey's eyes fixed on Logan. She shivered to see the look of pure hatred peeping through the well-rehearsed mask of civility, and for the first time, she began to conceive a fear of Mr Grey. He did not know she had seen him; his attention was too fiercely fixed on Logan.

She tried her best to shake off the uncomfortable sensation and maintain her usual liveliness of spirit. But she was not happy, and she was glad when the guests had gone.

When the family retired for the evening, Isabella did not go straight to sleep but instead slipped out of her own room and went next door to her sister's. She tapped lightly on the door; hearing her sister bid her enter, she went in.

Maria turned towards the door. She started as she saw her sister.

'Why, my dear Isabella!' she cried. 'How pale you are. You look dreadfully wan. My poor darling, are you unwell?'

'No, I'm not ill, Maria, but something is troubling me.'

'Come,' said Maria patting the bed. 'Sit by me and tell me what it is.' Isabella joined her sister and began to tell her of her fears.

'Did you see the way Mr Grey looked at Mr Logan tonight? He looked as though he hated him,' said she. Maria smiled.

'Well, in the circumstances it would be natural enough; Mr Logan did, after all, abscond with your affections and callously steal you away from him,' she teased.

'Oh, don't say so! To say he stole me from him makes it sound as though I were his property somehow.'

Maria, seeing her sister's evident distress, ceased to tease her and endeavoured instead to soothe her.

'My poor dear; whatever is the matter?'

'I am afraid, Maria, dreadfully afraid! You did not see the way he looked at him. It was so utterly malevolent. I really believe that he intends some evil toward Mr Logan.'

Maria was taken aback by this pronouncement, but something in her sister's voice impressed her.

'Do you know what you are saying, Isabella? Surely, you do not truly believe that he means to harm him?' she asked in hushed tones.

'I do not know. I cannot explain it, but I have this awful feeling that something dreadful is going to happen. A kind of presentiment if you will.'

'There is certainly something strange about Mr Grey,' said Maria thoughtfully. 'His eyes are always so cold, almost empty. I know I should not care to be married to such a man. I pray that you are wrong, Isabella; but I do not see what is to be done.'

'I must warn Jack.' She blushed. 'That is, Mr Logan.'

'But he will think it is only a woman's fancy. Men are so infuriatingly closed-minded,' said Maria throwing herself back on the bed.

'It cannot be helped. I cannot do nothing. I must tell him and bear his ridicule.'

As it turned out, Mr Logan took her words very earnestly. Unbeknownst to her, he too had seen the look on Grey's face and was not unimpressed. He promised her most sincerely that he would take particular care when it came to Grey.

However, undeterred by Grey's jealous attentions, he determined to pursue his hopes and to make her an offer of marriage. The offer was made, and she very readily accepted. Her parents made no objection, and there was great rejoicing. For a day or two, it seemed Grey's oppressive influence was lifted. Isabella and Maria were so distracted that they hardly spared a thought for Mr Grey.

Then one morning their father returned from town with the news that he had seen and spoken to Mr Grey. All at once, Isabella's fears were recalled to her.

'He had heard of Isabella's engagement and wished to offer me his congratulations,' her father was saying.

'That was very kind of him, I'm sure,' replied her mother.

'Kind? Pah!' cried her father, much to everyone's surprise. His wife and daughters stared at him, waiting for him to elaborate on this exclamation.

'There was nothing kind about it. Oh, he was civil enough, I grant you, and his tone of voice perfectly pleasant; but the look in his eyes!' He checked himself. He cleared his throat. 'Still, I suppose a little bad feeling is to be expected under the circumstances. All the same though, I think I'm glad that you decided against him, my dear,' said he to Isabella.

'A nobler man would have been content to see her happy if he truly cared for her,' said Maria.

'Quite right,' agreed her mother.

'Well, well, perhaps he will, once his wounded pride has healed,' said Mr Simpson. Isabella had remained silent during this exchange and was now very pale and still.

'Are you quite well, my dear?' asked her mother. 'You look dreadfully pale.'

'I am afraid I do feel rather unwell, Mama. If you will excuse me I think I shall retire.'

'Of course, my dear.'

***

She climbed wearily into bed. Barely had she pulled the covers about her before she was asleep. But if she had hoped that sleep would revive her she was to be disappointed. Her sleep was restless and disturbed. Dark, oppressive images plagued her dreams.

She awoke to darkness; in the still silence of the night, she could just hear the hall clock striking two. She found that she shrank from the darkness. For the first time since her early childhood, she grew afraid of the dark, fearing that which dwelt therein. As she lay alone in the empty silence, it was with a thrill of indescribable horror that she felt something like a cold hand brush against her cheek!

No sound of movement reached her. Whatever had touched her, in the total darkness there was nothing to tell her where it was, or what it was. She lay motionless, numb with terror. She wanted to scream out, but no sound came. She tried to throw herself from the bed, but her limbs felt heavy and unmovable.

Finally, her voice broke free of whatever power had bound it, and she screamed. Oh, how she screamed. It was a moment only before the door flew open, and her terrified sister stood framed in the doorway, bringing with her the welcome light of a candle. To the terrified Isabella she was the very image of an angel of mercy.

Maria was soon followed by their parents, for the screams had roused the whole household. With they brought the blessed relief of further light. Maria went straight to her sister and begged to know what was wrong. Clinging desperately to Maria, in great gasping sobs Isabella tried to make the source of her terror understood.

But no sooner had she stammered out the words than she became aware of it, in the flickering candlelight, one orphan shadow in the corner of the room. A shadow with nothing to cast it. It stirred, almost imperceptibly before seemingly melting away through the wall.

Crying out in her terror, she pointed to the corner.

'You see it! You see it! Oh, it is he; I know it is he.'

By now the poor girl was so hysterical that all their soothing and reassurances that it was only a nightmare were of but little use. Only when Maria promised to stay with her did she, at last, begin to be calm again. Eventually, she was overcome with the extreme fatigue that invariably follows such a heightened degree of anxiety. She fell into a fitful slumber.

Maria, however, did not sleep. Once she was sure her sister was asleep, she slipped from the bed and taking up her candle examined minutely the corner indicated by Isabella. Perhaps it was only suggestion, but she had fancied for a moment that she too had seen something in the corner. She ran her fingers along the wall where the shadow had been; it was strangely cold, far cooler than the rest of the wall. She held her candle forward. The flame was steady; there was no hint of a draught.

***

After that night, Maria continued to sleep in her sister's room, for Isabella had conceived a dread of being left alone after dark. She would often wake terrified and perspiring. In these moments the strong impression of there being some inhuman presence in the room returned to her, and she was overwhelmed by an oppressive sense of evil all about her.

The doctor prescribed a sleeping draught; but although it made her sleep, the dreadful sensations which had haunted her waking self now pervaded her nightly dreams.

Though her nights had taken on an unpleasant aspect, the excitement she felt at the arrangements for her upcoming marriage and the steady affections of Mr Logan did not allow her to be wholly depressed of spirit. However, as time went on, these nightly horrors began to take their toll. She became nervous and her pretty complexion became tired and careworn.

Such was the concern of her family and physician that a change of air was recommended to be undertaken at the earliest opportunity; the family, therefore, removed themselves to the seaside. At first, it seemed that the change of scenery had worked its cure upon her troubled mind. Every morning she would walk along the promenade with her mother and sister, and the blustery salt breeze brought back the colour to her pallid cheeks. Her sleep too became easier, and at the end of the first week, much of her liveliness of spirit was restored.

Her mother was inclined to believe that her daughter had suffered an overexcitement of her nerves, brought on by the preparations for the impending wedding; she held firmly to the belief that sea air and a little healthy exercise would soon mend matters. Isabella's continued recovery seemed to bear out her assertion.

At the end of that first week, her father left them for town, having business to attend to. He was to join them again at the end of the following week. Thus freed from the burden of male company, the three ladies decided to embark on a voyage of exploration to the shops of the town; the intention being to buy wedding clothes for the party and any other little necessaries for Isabella's new wardrobe.

They were strolling along when Maria drew her sister's attention to some item or other in one of the shop windows. Isabella turned and proffered her opinion, but as she did so she fell suddenly silent. Something else had caught her attention. Reflected in the glass she saw the figure of John Grey, watching her. She gasped, her breath catching in her throat.

She turned swiftly, but to her bewilderment, she saw no sign of him. She searched the faces of each passer-by, anxiously watching for that of her oppressor, but he was not there; he had vanished, melted away like a phantom, like the shadow in the corner.

***

After her fright in town, something of Isabella's former gloom returned. Her mother had told her not to be so silly; she had been mistaken; that was all. Besides, even if she had seen Mr Grey, it was hardly a matter of any concern to them and certainly nothing to work oneself up over. He was as entitled to a holiday by the sea as anyone else; was he not? What was Mr Grey to them or they to him? Isabella had made her choice, and there was nothing he could do about it.

Isabella remained unconvinced. Though her mother was not fond of Mr Grey she did not have the same horror of him which had daily grown upon her. She was convinced that somehow, she knew not how, he was responsible for her troubles; it was he who was behind the ominous shadow that haunted her room at night, for the evil dreams that plagued her. It was all the workings of his malice and bitter envy.

On her arrival by the sea, she had fulfilled a promise to her friend Miss Jefferies and written that young lady a letter assuring her of their safe arrival. She gave her particulars as to their lodgings, the town and the entertainments on offer.

The morning following the incident in town, she came down to breakfast to find a reply to this letter waiting for her. It struck her that when she wrote again it might just be worth her while to inquire of her friend whether Mr Grey were away from home at present.

Only after she had despatched her letter did she realise how futile was her inquiry. Even if he were still at home what comfort was there in that if what she suspected were true? She had, after all, sensed his presence in that strange shadow in her room where he could not have been, at least in his person. Despite her mother's efforts, her thoughts weighed heavily on her mind.

However, her father's return accomplished that revival of spirits which all her mother's reassuring words could not, for he brought with him the unexpected person of Mr Logan. Anxious for the health of his fiancée, he had journeyed at the earliest opportunity to call upon her.

What dark thoughts could remain in the presence of that wholesome, honest countenance? His presence was like a tonic to Isabella's fragile nerves. Such was her delight at his unexpected arrival that within half an hour all thoughts of Grey were swept away.

In the afternoon the party set out together to the beach. Isabella, on her fiancé's arm, felt she must be the happiest girl there. There was an amateur brass band competition taking place a little way up the beach, and the deep, cheerful melodies floating on the air delighted her. It was warm but not hot, and the gentle sea-breeze danced pleasantly about them. She sighed contentedly. The sense of serenity that she felt at that moment translated in her features to an almost ethereal beauty. Mr Logan looked upon his future bride with great admiration. They walked a little way behind the others, welcoming the chance of conversing unheeded.

'Do you like the seaside, dearest?' He asked her.

'Yes, exceedingly. There is something invigorating about the sea air; is there not?'

'Perhaps we shall take our honeymoon by the sea somewhere. Would you like that?' She smiled at him warmly. It gave her such joy to think of their future happiness.

'I should like that very much,' she answered.

'Oh, what a day it will be when I may call you my wife. I declare, I believe you have made me the happiest man alive, my dear Isabella.' She blushed very prettily at the compliment.

Their attention was drawn for a moment to the band. As they listened Logan was suddenly recalled to himself as he felt Isabella's hand tighten upon his arm. Her fingers held him in a vice-like grip. He looked at her in surprise. To his great alarm he saw that her face was deathly pale, her features rigid, all the former serenity was gone.

'My dearest Isabella! Whatever is the matter?'

'It is he! I know I was not mistaken. It was he; I am sure. He is here. I saw him in the crowd, only for a moment; but I saw him.'

'Saw who?' asked her fiancé in bewilderment.

'Mr Grey!' She turned to him and spoke in earnest tones. She poured out the whole story. She told him of all her definite fears and vague impressions, of all that had led to her current state of nerves. She held nothing back. He listened, his face growing grave.

'Do you think me mad?' she demanded.

'Of course not, my darling. But only think what you are saying, Isabella. I certainly do not trust Grey and I think him more than capable of mischief when moved to it; but what you are suggesting… that he has some kind of supernatural power, it is absurd. These shadows are just nightmares, my darling.'

'Then how am I to account for this dreadful feeling that he is continually watching us?'

'I have no doubt you are right to mistrust him, but it seems to me that his influence is natural rather than supernatural. I believe that your fear and mistrust of him has created such a strong impression that it has worked upon your nerves. That is all.'

'You really think so?' said she with a trace of relief in her features.

'I do.'

'I pray you are right.'

***

The following morning brought a reply from Miss Jefferies. She answered her friend's inquiry by assuring her that Mr Grey had not left the town. She also added that "he wore a very dark expression" when she had seen him last and had apparently given up all pretence of civility. He was, she remarked, "quite changed".

Isabella did not know what to make of this news. He had not left home and yet she had seen him twice since her arrival at the coast. Was it truly fancy, or could this man really have some kind of extraordinary and villainous power? She suspected the latter but if that were the case how could she hope to defend herself against such a force.

If he could spy upon her wherever she was, she could have no privacy, no respite; there could never be a single moment when she could be certain she was not under his observation. Even in the apparent safety of her room he had shown himself capable of intrusion, by she knew not what means. She saw no release from such subtle and hideous infamy.

It was with great reluctance that she bid farewell to Mr Logan when he had to return home, but the distress at the parting was in some way mitigated by the knowledge that they too would be returning in a very few days. She felt stronger for his presence, and in the hours immediately following his departure she cut a forlorn figure.

Alone in her room before dinner, she sat at her dressing table, looking sadly at her reflection. She looked tired. She felt tired; the preceding weeks had taken their toll.

She sighed and picked up her necklace from the dressing table and held it to her throat. The metal was cold against her skin, and she shivered as it touched her neck. The clasp was awkward, and she struggled for a few moments, becoming increasingly frustrated. She contemplated finding Maria or a maid to assist her.

Suddenly her frustration gave way to terror. This time it was not the touch of metal that caused her to shiver but the touch of hands! Cold, invisible hands took the necklace from her and fastened the clasp. She sat motionless, too terrified even to scream, as she felt the phantom fingers move around her throat; she thought they meant to strangle her, but after a moments pressure they released their grip and moved downwards, coming to rest on her shoulders. She felt their evil caress and a sensation as of breath against her neck.

Such was her terror in that moment that she would have surely fainted had not the door opened and Maria entered. The hands let go, and the presence retreated. She flew into her sister's arms sobbing wildly.

She did not tell her parents of her experience. They would be sure to worry. They would convince themselves that her mind was unsound, that she was mad or hysterical. Maria was her only confidant, the only one she could trust; she knew she would keep her secret.

She could not risk being deemed unfit to proceed with the marriage. No, she would not allow that. For she thought that whatever Grey's means of harassment his aim at least was clear, to prevent the marriage and to take possession of her. That, she could not countenance.

Though she was determined that nothing would prevent the wedding, she did harbour fears for Mr Logan. So far, Grey's attention seemed to be on her. Though he had as yet caused her no actual harm, the woman he was believed to love, what might he do to the man who stood in his way?

**

The night of their return home, her dreams were filled with vivid and hideous visions. She dreamt of her fiancé lying dead in her arms, his eyes open in the cold, glassy stare of death. In the dream she wore a wedding gown; it was spattered all over with his blood. The blood dripped from her hand, the wedding ring upon her finger smeared with it. Her tears fell and mingled with the pools of crimson. She awoke from that nightmarish tableau, cold and perspiring, in the early dawn. In her agony, she cried aloud for deliverance.

Maria stirred beside her. Blinking and confused, she sat up and inquired with great concern whether her sister had suffered another nightmare. Isabella fell upon her sister's shoulder sobbing. When at last Maria could make sense of her sister's broken speech, she grew very grave.

To Isabella's great comfort, she did not dismiss her fears as fancy or the dreams of an over-active and excitable imagination.

For a moment Maria had hesitated, unsure whether her sister's state of mind would be the better or worse for her confessing her own misgivings. In the end, she decided that Isabella would take more comfort from knowing herself to be believed and understood than she would from insincere reassurances. So, she told her of her own experiences on the night of the first alarm, how she too felt, with an indescribable sense, that there was something at work that she did not understand.

Indeed, Maria could not accept their parents' casual dismissal of the situation. Isabella was not of a flighty or fanciful disposition; she was in fact just the opposite. Of the sisters, Isabella had always been the more level-headed and rational of the two, but both were sensible girls.

The sisters expected and preferred adventures to take place only within the pages of books; when the cover was closed they expected them to remain where they were and not to trouble the everyday business of their lives. Now, here they were at the very centre of some macabre and grotesque mystery. They decided that come the morning proper they would pay a visit to the church.

As soon as breakfast was over they went out. Though they were greatly afraid of seeing Mr Grey, they walked on with purpose. The vicar received them warmly and with great cordiality. Isabella told him something of her plight, of the dreams and of the sense of oppression but she did not tell him all that she might have done. Her confidences were vague and she never mentioned Mr Grey nor the power he had over her. The vicar spoke comforting words and promised prayers. There was little advice he could give her other than to pray and believe that God would deliver her. So she prayed, and Maria prayed.

That afternoon Isabella and Maria set out together to walk over to the hall, to take tea with Miss Jefferies. The most direct route, which they were accustomed to take, was via a small plantation which lay between the two houses; there was a gate on one side opening into the Simpson's garden and one on the other which opened onto the driveway of the hall. As they approached the hall gate they saw something moving amongst the trees. Isabella's heart leapt. Was it Grey? The sisters clung to each other, expecting the worst. Then the source of the movement became clear as a young girl stepped into view from behind the trees. Isabella almost laughed aloud with relief.

The child smiled at them. Such was the warmth and innocence of the girl's expression that the sisters could not help but return her smile. She was dressed simply but neatly, and Isabella thought she was perhaps the daughter of one of the servants at the hall; she could not recall ever having seen the child in the town, which seemed strange in so small a community. Of course, it was possible her family were new to the town or only visiting.

They walked forward towards the gate. When they came up beside the girl. Isabella stopped to speak to her.

'You gave us quite a start, child.' The child bobbed politely.

'I'm very sorry, ma'am.'

'That's all right. I'm afraid we're interrupting your play,' said she kindly.

'No, ma'am I wasn't playing. I'm on an errand.'

'Oh, I see. Then we mustn't keep you.' The child looked at her very curiously then said,

'There is a shadow at your back ma'am. They do not see it, but it is there. You can feel it?'

Isabella stumbled back a step, shocked by the child's words. She heard herself responding as though across a great distance. The words came unbidden by her.

'Yes, I do.'

'There is danger.'

The child reached into a pocket of her dress and removed an object, which shone as it caught the light. She held out her hand to Isabella, with the object lying on the open palm. It was a silver disc, about the size of a florin, with a single hole near the edge; gemstones in a rainbow of colours formed the shape of an eye on the surface of the disc. The stones winked in the afternoon sun; there was an almost mesmeric air about the object. The child spoke again.

'Take this amulet and give it to the one you love. It will shield him from harm.'

'Amulet?'

'Yes, it will protect him. Those who seek to commit evil against him will find it turned back upon themselves. Take it.'

Isabella took the disc cautiously from the girl. It was cold, and it seemed to emit the merest suggestion of a vibration through her hand. For a moment she wondered if this was a trick by Grey to bring some evil upon them, but such was the feeling of love and protection that she felt from the amulet and the mysterious child that she dismissed the thought at once.

'Thank you,' said she. 'But you must let me pay you for it. How much?' She reached into her purse and with the help of Maria, for her hands were shaking badly, she managed to produce a handful of coins for the child, unsure of how much such an item might be worth.

The sisters looked up expecting the child's response; they were amazed to see that she had gone; but where had she gone? There was no sound or movement amongst the trees, and though they searched for some time they could find no trace of the girl.

Much perplexed, they continued on to the hall. Over tea the sisters made inquiries as to whether Miss Jefferies knew who the child might be; they did not mention the amulet. They would have liked to have found the girl and given her some remuneration, but Miss Jefferies did not know.

'There are,' said she, 'several children on the estate who might easily match such a description.'

There was little more they could do but hope to meet the child again in the plantation or in the street.

The evening brought Mr Logan to them. Though the young couple were, of course, pleased to see each other, the young man was not in his usual humour.

When they inquired as to whether something were the matter he gave this account,

'I am afraid I have had a rather trying time of it since I saw you last. It began when I was on my way home from the coast. I was waiting on the platform when I felt a sudden force at my back, as though someone had pushed me; I nearly fell onto the rails just as the train was coming in. If it had not been for the man beside me grabbing me I would have fallen. I looked about me, but in the crowd, it was impossible to see who it might have been. It must have been an accident, of course.'

Isabella was greatly alarmed to hear this tale. It seemed all her fears were coming to pass. Her father spoke.

'Extraordinary business! But you say that's when it began; there is more to tell then?'

'Yes, I am afraid so. The train journey itself was uneventful, and I reached my destination unharmed. It was when I was on my way back home from the railway station that the next incident occurred. I was halfway back to town when suddenly the horses stopped dead and reared up violently. It was all my driver could do to prevent them from bolting and overturning us. It was lucky for us that we were not travelling at any great speed when the alarm occurred, or the damage might have been far worse. Jones, my driver, had all on to calm the beasts. He said something must have frightened them. We thought perhaps some animal had run out in front of them and startled them, but Jones had seen nothing, and we found nothing.'

'Well,' said Mr Simpson, 'horses can be skittish and take alarm at a little thing like a sudden noise or a shadow in a lonely spot.' Isabella shuddered.

'I expect you are right,' said Logan. 'All the same, they were more than nervous; the poor creatures seemed absolutely terrified. It was a good fifteen minutes before we could persuade them to pass the spot. Jones was inclined to believe the place must be haunted!' He laughed at the idea of this. 'I told him not to be a fool. Besides, I've never heard of such a thing as a ghost on that stretch of road.'

'Indeed not,' said Mr Simpson.'

'But it didn't end there. That night I nearly dropped a lamp and set the house alight; then the following morning I tripped on the stairs going down to breakfast and sprained my ankle. Then I almost choked on my food. The list goes on. I really have had the most extraordinary run of bad luck.' Maria stole a sideways look at her sister.

'Dear me,' said she. 'You seem to have had a very bad time of it, sir.'

'Indeed, but I suppose these things are sent to try us. Still, no harm done.'

Isabella did her best for the rest of that evening to portray a lightness of spirit which she did not feel. When Mr Logan rose to leave them she went to see him out. Once they were in the hall she detained him a moment.

'There is something I wish you to have,' said she.

'A present is it?' said he smiling broadly.

'Yes, it is just a small token. But it would mean so much to me if you would take it.'

'How could I refuse you anything, my dearest?'

'You flatter me, sir,' said she shyly. Then, holding out her hand she presented him with the amulet.

'Hello! What's this? It's rather an unusual piece isn't it? Very skilfully done. In this light, it looks almost like a real eye, apart from the colours of course. What a strange illusion.'

'I was told it was a kind of good luck charm.'

'Well, after the last few days I could certainly use a little of that.'

'Then you will keep it?'

'I shall keep it with me always, to remind me of you.' He made her a little bow and took his leave. She made a silent prayer that the amulet would keep him safe.

***

The days passed, and the frequency and severity of the unfortunate incidents which had dogged Mr Logan decreased until it seemed his run of bad luck had finally ended. But the evil influence which had exerted itself was not yet finished with that young man.

Two days before the wedding, the Simpsons were to dine with Mr Logan at his residence. The evening being a pleasant one, they had their driver drop them at the bottom of the drive, and they walked up to the house.

In the early evening shadows, they saw a figure standing before the house. As they came nearer, they could see that it was their host. Then, they saw some movement from another quarter. Something stirred in the bushes beside the house.

The movement became more distinct; in a moment one of the shadows cast by the bushes seemed to detach itself from the rest; it grew strangely and seemed to reshape and reform until it was something akin to the shape of a man.

The party on the drive had stopped in their tracks, halted by the sudden dread of what they were seeing.

Their host stood with his back to the bushes, apparently unaware of the unfolding horror behind him and the danger in which he lay.

Something must have alerted him, however, for in an instant he had turned and was now face to face with the formidable shadow. The ghastly apparition reached out a hand towards the throat of its victim. Logan began to choke. The shadow hurled him against the wall, all the while tightening its diabolical grip upon him.

Isabella screamed. The spell that held the family was shattered and they were running, running with all their strength to reach the unfortunate man.

Mrs Simpson flew into the house to get help. Mr Simpson sought to pull Logan from the grip of his monstrous aggressor. Then, some unseen force flung Mr Simpson back. He fell unconscious at his daughters' feet. They quickly stooped down to attend to him.

Isabella looked up to where her fiancé was struggling with the shadow. Logan's face was red and his resistance becoming weaker.

'Look!' she cried out as she pointed towards them. Her father, who had by this time come round, and Maria stared in amazement. The shadow's grip was loosening. Then Isabella noticed it. The amulet she had given him was hanging on Logan's watch chain; it seemed somehow to be drawing the shadow to it. More than that, the shadow was diminishing, draining away into the amulet.

Finally, the shadow faded to nothing, and Logan crumpled to the ground, breathless and exhausted. Isabella rushed to his aid. By this time Mrs Simpson had returned with the servants. Brandy was administered and a doctor sent for. In a very short while, Logan was sufficiently recovered that he was able to sit up and speak. He rubbed his throat.

'How am I to account for this?' asked he hoarsely. 'I cannot understand it. There was such a sense of malice in the thing, whatever it was.'

'Mr Grey,' whispered Isabella. Logan's eyes widened.

'The shadow in your room?'

'I believe it is he who has been persecuting us both all this time. He is wickedly jealous.'

'Can it really be? But if it truly is Grey who is behind all our troubles then how did he manage it? That's what I don't understand. What was that thing?'

'I do not know, but you are safe now and that is all that matters.'

'But will he try again?'

'I do not think so. It is odd, but I feel suddenly free; as though his power over us has gone.' Then a thought occurred to her. 'The amulet!' she cried.

'Amulet? Oh, you mean the charm you gave me.'

'Yes, I thought you might think a good luck token sounded less fanciful than an amulet; but you see I was terribly afraid for you.'

'My poor Isabella. I should never have doubted your instincts. I promise that when we are married I shall be a wiser man. Now let's have a look at it. Good heavens!'

'What is it?'

'Look.' He took the amulet from his watch chain and handed it to her. The gemstones which formed the image of the eye had changed colour; no longer did they shine with the colours of the rainbow, instead they were now a glistening and brilliant black.

***

It remains only for the sequel to this strange tale to be told. News reached them the following day that Mr Grey's valet on entering his master's room that morning had discovered him sitting fully clothed at his desk, cold and dead.

He had evidently died sometime the previous evening. It seemed he had retired early to his room having given the servant the night off and so was alone at the time of death. There were signs of blood about the nose of the dead man, and the doctor suspected a haemorrhage; Mr Logan and the Simpsons had their own ideas about what had caused the unexpected death, but they kept them to themselves.

Amongst the late Mr Grey's possessions were found a good many books that the God-fearing people of the town thought very questionable and entirely unwholesome. No further elaboration can be given on this point, for as soon as they could those same God-fearing locals saw to it that the books were burned, 'cleansed by fire', as they put it.

The wedding of Mr Logan to Isabella Simpson went ahead with no further impediment; they still possess the blackened amulet, and perhaps one day they will tell their children how they came to have it.

But to this day, no trace have they ever found of the mysterious child who was the means of their deliverance.

A Most Unusual Disturbance

It was early in my literary efforts that I found myself suffering from that unfortunate affliction which at one time or another befalls all those who entertain literary aspirations; in short, I found that my mind and my pen were not of one accord and would by no means of effort on my part be reconciled. I was on the verge of throwing in the whole enterprise as a bad job. Had it been one of the winter months I fear I may have condemned my efforts to the fire in my consternation; however, as it was a warm day in May, I instead contented myself to take an early evening stroll and leave my papers to their own fate.

Before very long the fresh evening air had done something to revive my flagging spirits. With my mood somewhat restored and the light beginning to ebb, I turned homeward. As I approached my own door again I was lost in thought, and it was a moment before I became aware of someone calling my name. Suddenly broken from my reverie, I glanced up and was greeted by the smiling face of my old friend Charles Fairburn.

'Ah, Hunter!' said he, 'I thought for the moment you had not seen me.'

'I confess I did not,' said I, 'for I was quite lost in thought.'

'I was just on my way to call on you, but if now is inconvenient...?'

'By no means! I would welcome the distraction.' Once settled in my study, I proceeded to relate to Fairburn the cause of my distraction.

'Ah ha!' cried he. 'Then it may be that my coming is fortuitous. I have it in mind to take myself away from town for a few weeks and take a little country air. I came to inquire if you would care to join me. You know how I tire of my own company after more than a few days, and I believe that such a change of atmosphere may be just what you need. What say you? Will you come?'

'My dear fellow, nothing would give me greater pleasure. I believe you are right, a little country air may be all that is needed to set me back on an even keel.'

'Excellent! Then I shall make the arrangements forthwith; that is if you have no objection?'

'Not at all, I can be ready in a very short time.'

So it was that a week later, in the company of my friend, I found myself in __shire. The first few days of our trip were uneventful, and I will spare the reader the unnecessary details of these.

One afternoon, shortly after luncheon, on the fourth or fifth day of our retreat, we were seated in the common sitting room of the inn in which we were staying. It had been agreed upon that the day being a warm one we would pass a while in reading and venture out a little later when the heat was not so great. Neither of us, however, could settle to our books, and it came to pass that we fell into conversation with another guest.

He was a young man by the name of Arthur Falkirk; he was tall and thin, with quick alert eyes and an amiable disposition. It transpired during the course of our conversation that, due to the death of his uncle, he had recently found himself in possession of the local manor house, which resided in a small estate just beyond the village. With so fine a house at his disposal, I wondered at his staying at the local inn. Possibly our faces displayed some trace of our surprise, for he was quick to explain.

'You will think it odd no doubt that I choose to take my lodging here when I have a house of my own so near at hand. The truth is gentlemen that I have not slept a night in that house since it came into my possession.'

'You do not care for the house then?' I inquired.

'Dear me no; it is not that at all; it is a most pleasant house, and it will be a fine home. I have in fact spent several nights there, but I tell you it is impossible to sleep there, and that is the mystery of it.'

'Ah ha!' exclaimed Fairburn, leaning forward with interest. 'A mystery is it? Then you must tell us all about it, for Hunter here is a collector of mysteries.'

'Is that so?' inquired our companion good-humouredly. I confessed that it was indeed the case. 'Then this may be just in your line, sir,' he said turning to me, 'if you would care to hear it?'

'Certainly, I would,' said I, with some enthusiasm.

'Well then, the matter is quite simple to explain; it is just this; every night when I retire I am the sole occupant of the central block, the bedrooms in the wings being either occupied by the servants' quarters or subject to repairs.

'On my first night in the house, I retired to bed at my usual hour. At first, all seemed well, but then around Midnight, I was awoken by the sound of music coming from within the house, a violin to be precise. At first, I was inclined to believe it was some mischief on the part of some of the servants; but the following morning, when I questioned them upon the point, they were most vehement in their denials. In fact, they were as surprised as I, and it is my belief that they thought me either dreaming or else mad. I was at first inclined to agree with the former assumption; now I wonder if it is not the latter, for every night I have spent in that house I have been subjected to the same disturbance.'

'Did you make no attempt to find the source of the disturbance?' asked Fairburn.

'Oh indeed I did, and that is the strangest part of it. As I said before, I was inclined to think it some mischief on the part of one or more of the servants; so, when I heard the music again, I arose and set about following the sound to its source. It did not take me long to trace the noise to the gallery on the floor below. The house is of a sturdy construction, and I was rather surprised that the sound should travel at such a volume to the floor above.'

'No doubt the miscreant made the same assumption,' said I.

'Ah! That was my thought exactly. Well, I thought it best to remain unobserved, to begin with, but the sound of the music covered my footfall easily enough. Well, gentlemen, imagine my surprise when I opened the door and found nobody within the chamber, yet the music played on!'

'You are quite sure that the music was still playing from within the room itself?' I asked in some surprise.

'Oh, quite certain, for the sound was very clear. Well, you can imagine I was a good deal puzzled by this. I am not by nature a nervous man, but I must admit I was somewhat shaken. I was on the verge of returning to my own room, and putting a good distance between myself and the disturbance, when I fancied...' He broke off here, shifting in his seat and glancing uncomfortably from one to the other of us.

'Do go on,' I prompted. 'You may speak freely.'

'Well, the fact of the matter is, as I turned to leave I thought I saw, from the corner of my eye, undefined shapes moving in the darkness. Then I sensed, rather than saw, that I was not alone; it was the most peculiar feeling, as though there were people all about me.' His eyes widened in recollection. 'I was greatly surprised by this and not a little alarmed; I turned to look full upon them..., and again there was no one there. Well, I was back in my bed before I was even aware that I had moved. So it has been every night since, though I have only ventured once more upon my nocturnal investigations.'

'And the result?' asked Fairburn, his attention piqued.

'Precisely the same,' replied our acquaintance. 'Even now, I am inclined to wonder if I am not the subject of some dreadful recurring nightmare or hallucination.'

'Well!' said I, 'this is a strange business indeed. Tell me though; have you had this *dream* since you have been staying at the inn?'

'No, I have not,' said he. 'Perhaps it is something about the house that suggests things to my mind, but I could not say what. It can, surely, only have been a dream and yet ...'

'There is only one way to determine the truth,' proclaimed Fairburn. 'If another person were with you at the hour of disturbance then it would offer you some corroboration of one theory or the other.' Our companion fell into thought for a few moments.

'Yes,' said he at last, 'the more I think on it, the more I am convinced; it is the only way. Alas though, I do not think it would be right to approach any of the servants with the matter. I wonder, I know it is a terrible liberty after so short an acquaintance, if you gentlemen would be prepared to join me in a vigil? I am new to the area, and it is desirable to me not to encourage whispers of madness amongst the locals. As you are a collector of mysteries, sir,' he said addressing me, 'you may find something of interest in the matter.'

'I'd be delighted!'

'We could easily arrange to be with you this evening, if it is convenient to you,' said Fairburn.

'Indeed, that would suit me admirably, for the sooner it is accomplished the sooner I hope to put my mind at ease.'

So, it was settled that we would dine with our new acquaintance and spend the night at the manor house. We left word at the inn that we had been called away and would be absent until the morning.

We spent a pleasant evening looking over the house and grounds, which were of a very pleasing aspect. After dinner, our host showed us to the scene of the recent disturbances. It was a relatively short gallery, filled with family portraits of various generations of his ancestors, some of whom peered down sternly at us from the frames as though we were the ones on display. Several windows, spaced at regular intervals along the wall, gave on to well-kept gardens. About halfway along the room, I noticed something which caught my attention.

'Hello!' I cried. 'What's this?' Painted on the external wall was a remarkably detailed representation of a door with a violin hung upon the back. Although it was a painting, I had at first mistaken it for a real door, so lifelike was the picture; so exquisite was the detail that the illusion was almost perfect.

'Ah,' said our companion, 'it is a curious feature is it not? I believe it was done during my grandfather's time, but save for that I know nothing whatever about it.'

'It is certainly unusual,' said I, 'and shows a remarkable skill on the part of the artist.'

Once we had finished looking over the gallery we retired to our rooms and agreed to meet again at a quarter to twelve. The night was a pleasant one, with none of the uncomfortable heat of the day. The moon cast a silver-blue light across the gardens, which took on a most enchanting appearance. It was possible to imagine oneself as having stepped into some old world of magic and enchantment. I spent some time in contemplating the scene and then withdrew myself to a chair to read until the appointed hour. The time passed quickly, thanks in no small part to the comfort of my surroundings.

When the clock in the hall struck the quarter hour we were all three in position outside the main gallery door. Fairburn opened the door a sliver, just enough to permit us a restricted view of the gallery beyond. We positioned ourselves as best we could, to see what would unfold.

We jostled uncomfortably for some minutes, as we kept our silent vigil. I was in a state of intense expectation when we heard the clock strike the hour. I became gradually aware of a dim creaking sound coming from somewhere within the room. Squinting in the meagre light that entered from the hall, I was at first at a loss to pinpoint the source of the sound. Fairburn, however, was quicker than I, for I heard him utter an exclamation of astonishment. Grabbing my arm, he directed my attention to the painted door that we had admired earlier. To my utter amazement, I saw what I at first believed to be a trick of the poor lighting; the painted door was a painting no longer but as real as the one I found myself clinging to, and it stood ajar.

I could not doubt my eyes for long, however, as within the room several lights burst into life. I say several lights but in truth, I could not honestly say what manner of lights they were as they appeared to have no source. The room was lit as though by a hundred candles, but there was not a candle or lamp in sight.

Our companion drew away from the door, his eyes twitching back and forth uneasily. For a moment I thought him likely to faint, but he rallied himself and crept silently back to join us.

We watched with bated breath to see what fresh revelations our adventure might incur. One by one, a crowd of the most delicate and dainty people I have ever seen came tripping lightly through the door. They were small, and light of foot, and seemed to glide rather than walk upon the ground. One of the strange little people reached up to the door and pulled down the violin, which had undergone the same process of transformation as the door itself. The others gathered around him, giggling and hopping from one foot to the other and clapping their hands in excited little gestures.

All eyes were on the little man as he raised the violin under his chin and lifted his bow. He began to play the merriest tune I have ever heard, and soon all his companions were dancing and whirling around the room, some in partnership and others alone, moving freely and happily in a blur of joy and merriment.

When the tune came to an end they stopped and applauded the musician. He nodded and then proceeded to the next tune. This went on for some time, as we watched in silent awe from our hiding place until, finally, the music stopped; the violin was replaced on its hook, and the crowd, with little murmurs of disappointment, reluctantly made their way back through the mysterious door.

When all had returned to normal, we withdrew to the library to discuss the result of our nocturnal investigation. Falkirk was evidently searching for some appropriate comment to break the silence. He need not have distressed himself, however, as Fairburn did the honours.

'My word!' he exclaimed before he'd finished closing the door behind him. 'What did you make of that, gentlemen?' Falkirk's mouth gaped open but no words came to him, so he filled it instead with brandy.

'It is very singular,' said I, feeling the inadequacy of the statement even as I said it. At this point, Falkirk found his voice.

'It is madness; surely, this cannot be?'

'If it is madness, sir,' said Fairburn with a wry smile, 'then we are all party to it.'

'That is so,' said I. 'We all witnessed the scene.'

'But...,' said our companion uncertainly, 'what can it mean? Who or what were those people?'

'I have not the faintest idea,' said I. 'It seems to me that your best hope of discovering the meaning of this is to research as far as possible into the origins of that extraordinary door.'

'You are right,' said he. 'We shall question the servants in the morning; if there is any legend connected with the house they are more likely to know than I. If that sheds no light on the matter there are many old family papers here in this very library that may enlighten us.'

I need not take up the reader's time with lengthy accounts of our interviews with the servants. Even amongst the older household members, we could establish nothing beyond the fact that the door was painted during our host's grandfather's time. It seemed the gentleman concerned was, rather like me, much interested in folklore and the unusual. Our host entertained some hopes that the mystery might be solved along those lines and set himself to examining the family library and papers.

Sadly, his investigations yielded nothing during the course of our holiday, and we were obliged to return to town without the explanation we had hoped for. We received word some weeks later from Falkirk stating that he was not much further on in his search; but he had found a passing reference in an old letter to *"an artist of most unusual skill"*, whom his grandfather had met on a visit to Ireland.

The repairs having been completed, he was now resident in another part of the house. On the whole, he considered it best to leave the door well alone; it was causing no real harm, and he was loathe to stir up trouble for himself from unknown quarters. Pending any new enlightenment, I cannot help but agree with him. So, I am afraid, dear reader that I must leave you as perplexed as I myself. I can but hope that some more worldly soul than I may in time offer an explanation, which is at this time beyond me.

Reflections on a Malady

It was in the July of an exceptionally warm year that I received a letter from an old friend of my school days Mr Godfrey Edwards. Edwards and I had been, as boys, the very best of friends. Since then, however, I had seen him with lessening frequency. In consequence, when I received his letter it was full three years since I had seen him last. The intervening time had seen him marry and settle out of town. Circumstances had prevented my attending the wedding, so I had not as yet had the opportunity of meeting his bride.

So, when I received his letter inviting me to stay with them for a few days I very readily assented. Having nothing very pressing on hand, I wrote that I could be with him as soon as he wished. A date was, therefore, fixed upon, and a very few days saw me in a first-class carriage bound for a pleasant weekend with some excellent company, in the fresh country air. Nothing could have been pleasanter to my mind at that time.

The afternoon of my arrival was hot and humid, and the air was heavy. As I stepped down from the train and made my way through the various gatherings of passengers, I chanced to see my friend waiting for me upon the platform.

'Hunter!' cried he amiably, stepping forward to greet me. 'My dear fellow, I cannot tell you how delighted I am to see you again.'

'And I you, Edwards; it has been too long.' As we shook hands, I took the opportunity of observing my friend; I was surprised to see that despite his outward cheerfulness something was evidently amiss. As long as I had known him, he had always been meticulous as to his personal appearance; he was always neat and clean shaven; now, however, his clothing was fastened awry, his chin was unshaven and he had a general unkempt appearance. His face too was pale and drawn and his eyes dark and sunken. This was not the face of the lithe and active man I had known. I was about to question him upon the point when he took up my bags and began to lead me away from the station.

He had a dogcart waiting, and we settled ourselves for the short drive to the house. So, in the uncomfortable afternoon heat, we began our journey over pleasant country roads. I was struck at once by the vibrancy of colour before me, which is so sadly absent in town. The fields and hedgerows were alive with all the bustle of nature. It seemed as though every flower in the place had sprung up to greet my arrival. I could not imagine a more charming sight.

Edwards did not speak for some minutes. He seemed completely unmoved by the surroundings and the occasional remark that I let fall upon the subject. Not wishing to press him, I waited patiently and contented myself with admiring the beauty of our surroundings. I fancied, more than once, that he was on the verge of making some communication, but he checked himself each time.

'You think me much changed,' said he suddenly. I was somewhat taken aback by this sudden interjection.

'You do not seem to be quite yourself,' said I cautiously.

'Ever the diplomat, Hunter,' he laughed. 'A less tactful man would suppose that married life does not agree with me,' said he with a half-smile, 'but I assure you, nothing could be further from the truth.' I said nothing; I waited instead until he should continue.

'You have not yet had the pleasure of meeting my wife,' said he, 'but I feel certain that when you do you will agree that a kinder or more generous-spirited woman would be hard to come by.'

'I am sure I shall,' said I good-humouredly. 'You have always had the best of taste, Edwards, and what is more, the very best of luck,' I laughed.

'Ah!' cried he, 'you may say so; until recently I would have readily agreed with you.'

'And now?' I asked.

'Oh, I consider myself very fortunate. Nevertheless, we have had our troubles, but I believe we are back in the sunshine now.'

'I am sorry to hear you have been troubled.'

'It has been a trying time, to be sure. Elizabeth was taken ill with a fever during the winter. More than once her life was despaired of. Even now she is not quite so hearty as before, but she is in all other respects quite recovered.'

'My dear fellow, why did you not tell me? If that is the case, are you sure my visit will not be an imposition? I can very easily return to the station and catch the next train back to town if it is too soon,' said I. My friend seemed genuinely surprised by my suggestion, for he hastened to reassure me that my presence was the very thing that he particularly desired at that moment.

'No, no you mustn't go. I won't hear of it. We would not have dreamt of inviting you if it were inconvenient in any way! That would make us fine hosts would it not?' asked he smiling. 'Besides, Elizabeth is looking forward to meeting you, and I am certain we will both be better for your company. We have been alone too long and we are ready for a little society.'

'Then I shall be the very spirit of polite society,' said I with a smile.

By then we were nearing the brow of a small hill, on a path which swept down towards the house. In the brief moment in which we were perched atop that hill, looking down on the house below, a feeling without name passed through me. I did not understand it then, though I have thought on it often since. Had I known then what awaited me, I may well have jumped from the cart and returned to town; as it was, even in my ignorance, it was with a sense of foreboding that I made that descent.

As we pulled up in front of the house I saw the figure of a woman, whom I took to be Mrs Edwards, framed in the doorway. Smiling, she came forward to greet us. She was a beautiful woman, tall, with golden hair and deep brown eyes. The dark circles beneath her eyes were the only hint as to her recent illness. Yet, despite her obvious charms, something about her appearance made me uneasy.

'Hunter, I'd like you to meet my wife, Elizabeth.'

'I am delighted to meet you, at last, Mrs Edwards,' said I, shaking her proffered hand. To my astonishment, her hand was cold to the touch, despite the heat of the day. I felt a shiver of ice crawl over me.

'And I you, Mr Hunter. Godfrey has told me so much about you. I'm so pleased you were able to accept our invitation,' said she, in a voice which was soft and possessed of a curious, far away quality. 'I hope you are not too fatigued from your journey. It is rather a warm day for travelling I'm afraid.'

'Indeed, but the beauty of this part of the world has more than compensated me for any slight discomfort I assure you.'

'Do come through,' said she, gesturing towards the door. 'I hope, once you are settled in your room, you will join us for tea?'

'I thank you, yes; a little refreshment would be most welcome.'

I was duly despatched to my room and left to prepare for tea. Once my preparations were finished, I took the opportunity to acquaint myself with the view from my quarters. My room looked out over the front of the house, and once again I was struck by the beauty of the landscape. I looked on in admiration. Edwards truly was a lucky man.

***

After tea, Mrs Edwards excused herself and retired to her room to rest for a while, so that I was left alone with

Edwards. We decided that, as the afternoon heat had subsided a little, we would take a short stroll.

We wandered through a little gate that led, via a gently sloping avenue of trees, to a small wood. We whiled away a pleasant hour, stopping briefly at the far end of the wood to admire the view; from there I could see out across the surrounding countryside, the graceful curve of the hills and the myriad shades of green, glowing with a pink and golden haze in the late afternoon sun. A few white clouds drifted lazily by. It was a scene which brought a sense of serenity to my mind, a sense which I carried with me still as we approached the house once more. However, my peace was unexpectedly shattered as we came towards the door, which flew open as we approached. A young maid came hurtling through it, at top speed, screaming; so intent was she on fleeing the house that she very nearly collided with us.

She stared at us, seemingly unsure now of whether she had not more to fear outside the house than in. She was undoubtedly in a state of terror and was shaking violently.

'Why, my girl,' said I, 'whatever is the matter?'

'Begging your pardon, sir, but I was so frightened,' she stammered. 'Oh, sir,' said she turning to my friend, 'I saw her again, just now.'

'Her?' I looked to Edwards for explanation. He looked suddenly grave.

'The ghost, sir,' she jumped in.

'Ghost! My word, Edwards, you don't mean to say you have a ghost on the property, and you never told me?' I asked in some surprise. He scowled.

'It is a foolish notion that the servants have got into their heads, nothing more.'

'Tell me, my girl, what does this ghost of yours look like?' I asked.

'Well, sir,' said she, trying hard to keep the tremor from her voice, 'I've only seen her from behind, and glad I am of it! The thought of her eyes on me...,' she shuddered again. 'It fair turns me cold. But she's a woman all right; I'm sure enough of that. She's all in white, but she sometimes seems to have a sort of glow about her, an odd kind of light, if you take my meaning, sir.'

'I see, and you say you saw her just now?'

'Yes, sir, just outside the library. I caught sight of her, and for a minute I couldn't move, no more than if my boots had been nailed to the floor, sir. But then she started to turn toward me, and I took such a fright for fear of her looking at me that I lost my wits and made for the door.'

'Well, I propose to go in now and see if our mysterious visitor is still there.' With that, I entered the house; neither Edwards nor the maid moved to follow me. I made a brief examination of the ground floor rooms, looking for signs of the ghostly woman. I could see nothing untoward, but I did feel a curiously cold sensation as I approached the library door, as though the air had been somehow disturbed just in that area. It could perhaps have been a draught, but there was no apparent source, and I felt it only on that particular spot. I pushed the door open slowly and peeped inside; there was nothing there. With nothing tangible to report, I returned to Edwards and the maid.

'Well,' said I, 'there is no sign of your visitor now at any rate.' I fancy Edwards looked as relieved as the maid.

'You see, my girl,' said he, 'nothing but fancy. I suggest you go back inside and be about your work, and we'll say no more about this.'

'Very good, sir. Thank you, sir.' With that, she bobbed and scuttled off to resume her duties.

'Have there been many of these kinds of incidents?' I asked.

'A few, but only in recent months. The house has never had any reputation before, so far as I am aware.'

'There are no romances attached to it?'

'None that I have heard, and such stories are hard to suppress amongst country folk; they serve as entertainment in these out of the way places. Yet, the servants are convinced that there is something wrong in the house.'

'You set no store by it yourself?' I asked. His gaze strayed from me to the ground, as he ran his finger under his collar.

'How can I? I am a rational man, and rational men have no business believing in such follies.'

'I see.'

No more was said on the subject at that time, and the conversation turned to more pleasant topics. I had begun to see, however, some of the reasons behind the changes I had observed in my friend.

***

The night found me wakeful. I was tired, yet sleep eluded me. I had lighted my candle and made a vain attempt to read until I felt more inclined for sleep, but time and again my eyes strayed from the page as my mind wandered back to the day's events. I lay on my back, my eyes tracing the patterns in the wallpaper.

Eventually, I slipped from the bed and went to the window. I pulled aside the curtains and pushed open the window, allowing the blue-tinged moonlight to puncture the darkness and the cool night breezes to lap at my face. I gazed out upon the night and felt acutely aware, as so many before me must surely have done, of the smallness of my own existence. I wondered what the meaning of it all was. I pondered on life and death and that strange unfathomable region that lies between the two.

It had started to rain, but I remained at the window. I closed my eyes and let the tide of fresh night air wash over me, the chill water brushing against my cheek.

I knew she was there before ever I saw her. I could feel her watching me.

I turned around cautiously, uncertain of what awaited me. I saw her; I saw, with my own eyes, that which was not possible. This was no living woman, no mortal body, yet I knew her. Aye, I knew her, for the woman before me was Edwards's wife! Such a feeling as was upon me in that moment cannot be imagined. You have heard, no doubt, those tales in which the souls of the dead are said to walk abroad, but did you ever hear tell of the soul of a living person walking, split asunder from its mortal body? I can well imagine the answer.

I stood for several moments, staring in dumb incomprehension. She said nothing, nor did she move, but there was an irrepressible air of sadness about her, which communicated itself to me. Her eyes seemed to plead with me, but what could I do? What did she want? I was at a loss, paralysed by shock and confusion.

Finally, I found my feet and began to move towards her; at that, she turned slowly and drifted from the room, through the closed door! This did away with any doubts I may have held as to her incorporeal nature. I raced to the door and threw it open. There was no sign of anyone along the length of the passage.

Puzzled, and with an aching head, I returned to my room. I had no recollection of returning to bed, but, nevertheless, I awoke there in the early morning light. So, I had risen and opened the curtains and the window; that at least I knew to be true; the sunlight flooding through the open window told me as much.

I arose and closed the window. Despite the summer's heat, I felt a chill within me. Had I been subject to some hideous hallucination? Perhaps the cold and my nocturnal vision were symptoms of approaching illness. Could a fevered mind account for what I'd seen? In truth, I would have been glad if it were so, as strange as that may seem, for I feared that my experiences of the night boded ill, and I longed for a rational explanation.

Once I was dressed and my morning routine completed, I felt a little more cheerful. The chill had gone from me, and the uncomfortable heat of the previous day had given way to a day that was pleasantly warm and clear. The slight coldness I had felt was probably the result of sleeping with the window open, which was contrary to my usual practice. What then of the vision of Mrs Edwards? Could it really have been a dream? I felt by no means certain; it had felt real enough and horrible enough. So, it was with some trepidation that I went down to breakfast that morning.

I do not know what I expected, but I need not have feared. Both Edwards and his wife were in fine spirits, and we enjoyed a pleasant breakfast together. I could not refrain, however, once or twice, from casting a curious glance at Mrs Edwards. Perhaps I hoped, or even feared, to see some acknowledgement of her late-night excursion, but there was none. Dream or not, I felt a vague but persistent sense of foreboding.

***

Edwards and I spent a leisurely morning strolling over the countryside. We reminisced about our school days and later spent much time in examining the most recently acquired additions to his library; in short, we spent as carefree and as pleasant a day as two gentlemen at leisure may reasonably hope to do; in consequence of such a day, by the time we joined Mrs Edwards for tea on the lawn my spirits were fully restored, and I was as happy as any man has a right to be. Sipping lemonade in the shade of the trees, and breathing in the heady scent of the roses, all my earlier gloom was abandoned.

***

In the evening we were joined by some of Edwards's neighbours, Doctor and Mrs Phelps and their niece, who resided with them, Miss Jennings. When we were all assembled in the drawing room after dinner, I fell into easy conversation with Mrs Phelps and her niece. The former was a good-natured, jolly, little woman and was clearly much attached to her niece. Miss Jennings, for her part, was a striking and fragile looking young lady; her delicate, porcelain complexion looking all the paler for the darkness of her hair. Her eyes were the unusually intense blue of a dusk sky, and more than once I found my own being drawn to them. I liked the young lady's company; her conversation proved her to be an intelligent and spirited girl.

At some stage in proceedings, the general conversation turned towards the subject of dreams; given my experience of the previous night, you can be sure I became at once alert. It was a state which did not escape the young lady's attention, for I fancied that she looked at me curiously for a moment.

Once or twice her eyes seemed to stray towards Mrs Edwards, though her gaze did not appear to settle directly on her but rather on some point beyond her shoulder. I turned instinctively to follow her gaze, and for a moment I thought I saw some movement from that region, but it was a moment's impression only. I turned back and was suddenly aware that the girl's eyes were now fixed on me. She looked puzzled. As I turned to her, however, she looked away quickly, colouring slightly. There was no sign that the others had noticed any of what had passed. Mrs Edwards was addressing the Doctor.

'Do you know, Doctor, I had the strangest dream, just last night, which I am quite at a loss to divine the meaning of. It was night time, and I was wandering about the house, holding a candle. I felt strangely cold. I was conscious of how silent and still the house was, and I felt terribly alone. I came into this room and walked up to the fireplace. Holding out the candle before me, I peered into the looking glass; as I looked I saw that I had two reflections. One was my true reflection; the second was very pale and seemed to be standing at some distance behind me, watching me. Now, what do you suppose it could mean?'

While the Doctor was musing on the subject, I found my mind returning, once again, to my own dream, if such it was. I began to think that there must be some connection, something which I could not as yet see clearly.

This discussion, naturally enough, led on to the notion of prophetic dreams and thus to the topic of fortune telling. It transpired in the course of the conversation that Miss Jennings was known to indulge in the occasional reading of tea leaves. The idea of this soon took hold with our hostess, who was most delighted with the idea of having her own leaves read. The doctor shook his head and frowned.

'Oh now, Henry, it really is just harmless fun; what possible objection could you have to that?' demanded his wife.

'Very well; if you must,' said he resignedly. He added under his breath, 'there is no use arguing with a woman.'

'Oh no!' cried Miss Jennings. 'I shouldn't, really.' She looked distinctly uncomfortable. It seemed to me that I discerned a fleeting look of panic in the girl's eyes. None of my companions seemed to have noticed this momentary lapse, however. Edwards and the Doctor were making light of the follies of women, and the ladies were uttering encouragements.

'Nonsense! You know you have such a delightful talent for it. Now, don't you let Henry put you off. Men can be such bores when it comes to these matters,' declared Mrs Phelps cheerfully.

'Oh yes, please do, Louisa,' coaxed Mrs Edwards. 'Until a few weeks ago I wasn't sure I had a future at all! It would be most delightful to me to see a glimpse of what I can now look forward to.' She looked fondly at her husband.

'Absolutely, my dear. I must insist,' chorused Mrs Phelps. At length, the girl was persuaded, and the party gathered around. It seemed I was the only one who had noted the girl's genuine reluctance. Mrs Phelps had her reading first and was duly delighted with a future of prosperity and travel. My gentlemen companions declined to indulge in a reading; I, however, allowed myself to be persuaded. In truth, I welcomed any chance to closer study Miss Jennings; the girl intrigued me immensely. She looked into my cup and smiled.

'I see a bouquet, Mr Hunter; it is a lucky symbol, meaning a happy marriage.'

'My own?' I asked encouragingly, 'for you see I am but a humble bachelor.'

'That need not be a permanent state of affairs you know, old chap,' laughed Edwards raucously. He looked at me knowingly. When my reading was finished it was the turn of Mrs Edwards.

The room darkened slightly as a cloud drifted across the sun. I turned my attention back to Mrs Edwards, who had just completed her part of the ritual and had turned her teacup over to Miss Jennings to read. Looking at her then, I felt again that odd feeling of revulsion pass through me. I could not understand why, but a vague nagging sensation had insinuated itself into the back of my mind. Yet, try as I might, I could not define it. I felt a growing unease in the presence of my hostess.

Miss Jennings turned her eyes to the teacup. A curious expression passed over the girl's face. She trembled; her eyes flickering slightly. There was a sudden crash as the teacup fell from her hand. She leapt to her feet.

'I am so very sorry, Lizzie,' she cried. 'How dreadfully clumsy of me.' I looked at her with concern. She seemed suddenly drawn and anxious. 'I am so sorry,' she repeated.

She staggered slightly. Her already pallid features were now ashen, creating a stark and shocking contrast to the coal blackness of her hair. Mrs Edwards sprang up and laid a steadying hand on her friend's arm. The girl recoiled from the touch with such violence that she nearly fell. Her hands clutched wildly at her dress as she backed away. She shrieked,

'Do not touch me; I cannot bear it! What are you? Oh, mercy! What are you? It is unnatural, abomination!' The girl was quite hysterical. Even to the most hardened mind, it was a terrifying sight to behold. In an instant, she crumpled and fell, insensible, and it was only through a quick and instinctive reaction that I prevented her landing heavily upon the floor.

'Well caught, sir,' bellowed the doctor, rushing to the girl's aid.

'Doctor, what on earth is the matter with her?' demanded Edwards, springing to my side.

'Hysterical most likely, brought on by this nonsense,' said the doctor, indicating the teacups. 'Fetch me some water.' Edwards did as he was bid and returned in a very few moments with the water, which the doctor proceeded to splash onto Miss Jennings's face. Suddenly the girl's wild eyes opened, and she gasped but remained speechless, breathing heavily. Her eyes were wide and unblinking, cold and glazed. I wondered then if those eyes were even seeing; there seemed to be an absence of presence behind them. They were fixed on the looking glass over the mantle. For a moment my own eyes fell on it. I saw Mrs Edwards's reflections. Yes, not one but two reflections, just as she herself had described them. I recognised in that second image my visitor of the night before. I knew then that this was what the lady had seen in her own dream.

My horror must have been evident in my features, for Mrs Edwards wheeled around to view the source of my alarm; she saw it. She clasped her hand to her mouth but not before a choking cry escaped her. She stumbled back a few paces.

'What does it mean?' she asked in desperation. Her hand fell to her side, her fingers furling and unfurling. She began to reel. Edwards was at her side in an instant.

'What the deuce is going on here?' demanded the doctor. He left his niece to the care of his wife and went to the assistance of Mrs Edwards. He looked grave.

'She is burning with fever. Quick now, we must get her to bed immediately.' Suddenly, a dreadful rasping sound was emitted from Mrs Edwards, as she crumpled in her husband's arms. The doctor examined her carefully and stood slowly to meet our inquiring eyes.

'I am dreadfully sorry, my boy,' said he to Edwards. 'She is dead.' A violent sob broke out from Miss Jennings.

Mrs Edwards was duly removed to an upstairs room, the clocks stopped, and the mirrors covered. Edwards remained alone with his late wife, while the rest of the sombre party reassembled in the drawing room. We discussed the matter of where I should spend the night; in the circumstances, I thought it best that I should not remain in the house. The doctor was in the process of recommending a local inn to me when a sudden hoarse cry came from upstairs; it was Edwards.

The doctor and I started at once. We found my friend, pressed against the farthest wall of the room, staring at the bed containing the body of his wife. We turned our attention to the body and saw, to our utmost amazement, that the lady was breathing, some slight colour returning to her cheeks.

In a moment I had torn the covering from the mirror. I looked deep and saw again the secondary image. This time it was so close that I shrank back at the thought that it could reach out and touch me. It seemed to have taken on an agonised and desperate appearance.

The doctor, in conducting a fresh examination of the lady, concluded that she had suffered an attack of catalepsy. I was far from satisfied with this explanation; I could see, in that looking glass, what he could not.

'She is trapped,' announced a voice from behind us. I turned and saw Miss Jennings standing in the doorway, with the doctor's wife close at her heels.

'What do you mean?' I asked in astonishment.

'It is her time. Her spirit wants to pass over.'

'Louisa!' snapped the doctor.

'Then why doesn't it?' I asked, ignoring the interruption.

'Something is holding her here.' In unison we turned to Edwards; he returned our gaze uncomprehendingly.

'Don't be absurd,' he cried. 'It is nonsense. Why do you keep looking at that confounded mirror?' he demanded angrily. Miss Jennings grabbed his arm and turned him, with more strength than I should have given her credit for.

'Look and see,' she cried, taking hold of his arm in a firm grasp. 'Listen,' she hissed. I heard the melancholy cry of the wind and saw, as she touched him, a sudden and violent start of recognition in his eyes.

The next moment he was at his wife's side and whispering something, which was inaudible to us. He kissed her tenderly upon the head. A deep sigh came from the lady on the bed, and the colour drained from her like the ebb of the tide. In that instant, we were engulfed in a mighty gale, which rose up from nowhere with the power of a titan. The wind shook the shutters and slammed the door with such force that it shook the room. Then, all was silent. Time passed, but this time there was no doubt that the lady was dead.

What passed between husband and wife in that moment we shall never know, for within a week Edwards too was lost. He was found one morning in his library, a look of complete and utter peace on his face.

There was but one good thing to spring from the events of that fateful night. You will not be surprised to learn, perhaps, that Miss Louisa Jennings is now Mrs Hunter. Strong as our bond is, we have vowed that we shall never presume to stand between death and his quarry.

Lifting the Veil

One Christmas, my wife having been called away to attend upon an ailing relative, I found myself facing the prospect of spending the festive season alone; that was until I received an invitation to spend Christmas with my friend James Millbrook and his family at their house in the country.

It seemed that on hearing of my plight his mother had immediately ordered him to issue an invitation to me, though he assured me that it was more in the nature of a summons than an invitation. Indeed, he said that the good lady would "brook no denial". I very happily accepted.

So, with gifts in tow, I set out. It was the day before Christmas Eve, and snow had begun to fall steadily. I viewed the diminishing city through the snowy curtain of the train window. I felt very glad that I had not delayed my journey, for I suspected that the snow might soon make travel a far more difficult prospect.

The village where Millbrook's family resided was not very far from town and the cobbled streets soon gave way to the open fields and snow-covered hills of the surrounding countryside. Before long I was standing, luggage in hand, on the platform of the little country station. In the sharp winter air, my breath mingled in white clouds with the steam from the train as I made my way from the platform. A trap had been sent for me, and after a brief ride over country roads, I was deposited before a not over-large, square house of the classical style with a large pillared portico dominating the front. Its white stuccoed exterior seemed as one with the pale snow-capped hills behind.

Millbrook was in the hall when I entered; he came forward and greeted me warmly.

'The compliments of the season,' said he smiling broadly as he shook me by the hand.

'And the same to you,' I returned.

His mother came scurrying into the hall with voluble expressions of welcome and glad tidings, and in no time at all, I was swept up into the heart of that convivial family gathering. I could not have been made more welcome if I had been myself a member of the family.

On the afternoon of my arrival, my friend and I went for a walk by the river. He was justifiably proud of the landscape of his birth, and he wished to show me all the splendours of its winter aspect. Every so often he would stop and point out to me some landmark or feature of interest. It was indeed a beautiful sight. If ever magic existed in the world then surely it was in that place.

We passed over a little bridge where the snow which had come to rest on the parapets blew upwards in little powdery clouds at the gentle coaxing of the wind. Icicles were forming on the trees, and the air was fresh and sharp. It was in all respects the perfect image of an English Christmas.

As we walked along, conversing as we went, there was a terrible commotion behind us as a bird took flight with a loud screeching, probably alarmed by some animal or other. Startled, however, by the sudden noise, Millbrook turned in the direction of the disturbance. As he turned, his foot slipped on the frozen ground beneath him; before I could stop him he was sliding down the frozen bank of the river, clutching wildly for anything to stop his descent, tumbling heavily as he went. He plunged into the depths of the icy water below.

I was after him in an instant. I scrambled down the river bank, half running, half sliding. I could see at once that he was in difficulties. Throwing off my coat I dived in after him. The cold exploded through my body, its icy fingers seizing at my heart. For a moment I could not breathe; forcing the fog from my mind I pushed onwards. Millbrook was slipping beneath the surface of the water as I reached him. With all the strength I had left to me, I hauled him up and dragged him slowly and laboriously back to the bank.

Luckily for both of us, for the cold had taken its toll on me also, a passer-by had witnessed the accident and had by this time made his way to us. Between us, we were able to get my friend out of the water. He had lost consciousness and there was an ugly red mark on his head, already turning to an angry purple. He must have hit his head in the fall. I need not take up the reader's time with lengthy explanations as to how help was fetched and we were conveyed back to the house; suffice to say that it was so.

Though I myself was advised to spend the following days in bed as a precaution I was none the worse for my exertions; Millbrook, on the other hand, never having had the most robust of health, was a more serious case. He fell into the grip of fever. For three days he lay in a delirious state. On the third evening, that of Christmas Day itself, a general prayer of thanks went up in the house when the fever broke. So ended that particular passage. I returned to town and Millbrook, in time, made a full recovery.

***

It was some weeks into the New Year when my friend came to call on me at my lodgings. It was the first time I had seen him since Christmas, and I was heartily glad to see him. I observed him as he drank his tea by my fireside. Although he was, he assured me, quite recovered in every physical sense, it was evident to me that he was labouring under some great nervous strain;

the tell-tale rattle of his teacup in its saucer, the pale face, the restless eyes, all testified to the fact. He leaned forward with sudden urgency.

'There is a matter I must consult you on, Hunter,' said he.

'By all means.'

'Tell me, how long was I unconscious with the fever?'

'Why, surely you know this already? The accident was on the 23rd and you awoke on the evening of the 25th, Christmas Day.'

'Three days, no more. You swear it?'

'But of course!'

'Just so, and yet…'

'And yet, what?' I asked

'Yet, I would swear an oath that it was longer.' I smiled at this.

'Well, I dare say the fever altered your perception of time somewhat.'

'Perhaps so but… Do you believe in life beyond death?'

'I don't know,' I said in some surprise. 'I believe that there are many phenomena that are as yet beyond our understanding, more than science will admit to. But why do you ask?'

'Because I believe that I have been there!' I stared at him for some time with what I am afraid must have been a very stupid expression.

'Been there?' I queried in bewilderment.

'Yes, and for no less than a month.'

'A month?' He nodded. I eyed our teacups thoughtfully.

'I had best fetch some brandy,' said I. Once my friend had taken a little of the brandy he was less agitated and more ready for discussion.

'You say you were in a kind of afterlife whilst you were lying unconscious?' I asked with keen interest.

'Yes, or at least that is what I suppose it to be.'

'What was it like? Can you describe it?'

'It was a glorious summer. There were open fields and birds singing and such a sense of peace and freedom from care as I have never known before. But I was not alone in this paradise, for there were others and more particularly there was a young woman with me, and she was the most perfect creature I have ever known. We spent all our days together, laughing and talking, walking through the fields and picking fruit from the trees. Then we would lie on our backs in the grass and watch the birds overhead.' His eyes had taken on a misty, faraway look. He sighed wistfully. 'Since I awoke I have missed her terribly.' Returning to himself he coloured slightly and stared at his teacup.

'Remarkable,' said I, 'though, it may be no more than a fever dream.'

'It might', he acknowledged, 'and yet all my instincts deny it.'

'What then? You believe you have passed beyond the veil to some other level of existence and returned?' I queried excitedly.

'I do.'

'And what of this woman?'

'Ah,' cried he dolefully, 'I cannot even recall her name. But I believe that she was destined for me and I for her, that our souls are somehow entwined. What is more, I feel that I have always known it and yet could not until now remember it, as though the information were somehow suppressed within my mind. I feel absolutely certain that I shall see her again.'

'What you are saying is extraordinary,' said I. 'Have you told anyone else of this?'

'I have not; I have no desire to be incarcerated as a lunatic.' He smiled wryly. 'The clergy exults in the notion of life after death, but if a man were to claim to have seen it and returned, they would condemn him as a madman or to be under the influence of evil. No, I have told no one but you, and I beg that you will be so good as to say nothing, for the time being at any rate.' He smiled feebly.

'Of course, if that is what you wish.'

'It is, yet I had to share my story with someone and you are more open-minded than most people and take an interest in such things. I knew that you would not dismiss my story. I know that I can rely on your discretion.'

'Certainly, you may.'

'Well, I must be going, but I shall see you soon I hope.'

'Indeed.' I looked at him thoughtfully as he rose to leave; small beads of perspiration were standing out on his brow, and there was still something of that restless faraway look in his eyes which I had observed earlier. 'Take care of yourself and do not hesitate to send for me or call on me if I can be of any assistance,' I urged. He thanked me and took his leave.

***

Three days later I received a telegram; it bore the following message:

"Have seen her. Come as soon as able. Millbrook"

I did not waste much time in puzzling over the message. I packed a bag at once, made such arrangements as were necessary and by the following day I was once again on a train out of town destined for Millbrook's family home, where he was currently still residing. You may wonder that I responded with such haste, but ever since hearing my friend's strange story, I had suffered from a feeling of great restlessness, perhaps of premonition. His summons did not surprise me, but it did concern me.

I was greeted on my arrival by his mother. She was a different woman to the one who had greeted me so cheerily a few weeks earlier. She was quiet and bore a solemn countenance; the redness of her eyes told of a mother's grief. She led me in silence to her son's room. As she stood with her hand on the door handle she turned to me and said,

'I fear that he is gravely ill, but he will not allow me to send for the doctor. Please, please, Mr Hunter, try and talk some sense into him. I knew that he should not have been about so soon after his accident, but you know how wilful he can be, and now look at the result. Please, do what you can. Make him see reason,' she pleaded. I did my best to reassure her that I would do all I could. She pushed open the door and ushered me inside.

'Mr Hunter is here, James,' said she gently. Her son was seated, with a thick rug over his knees, before a homely fire, which was the one concession he had allowed his mother. He looked up eagerly on hearing my name.

'Hunter, my good fellow! I am very glad to see you.' His mother nodded to me and withdrew. Millbrook watched her go; as the door closed behind her he beckoned me over.

'Come, come, sit down.' I drew up a chair opposite him and sat down before the fire. What a sight he was. If he had been pale and anxious the last time I had seen him he was doubly so now. His skin had a curiously grey tinge to it, and his eyes were dark and heavy; he had evidently not been sleeping well. 'I have seen her,' he continued. His limbs were taut as he leaned towards me, his every nerve straining.

'Seen her where?' I asked.

'Here, in this room; she came to me in my sleep.' My heart sank, for I confess I suspected that my friend's sickness had returned and he was suffering from the dreams of delirium.

'A dream then?' I asked.

'No, no! That is, she came to me in my dream, but it was not truly a dream. The dream was only the method of communication.'

'And what did she say to you?'

'I cannot remember clearly; it is like a fog,' said he. His eyes sparkled feverishly and he spoke with fervour.

'But she wants me to come to her. I know that with absolute certainty.' I looked at his furrowed brow and sunken features and frowned.

'That's as may be but you are unwell; you should be in bed. And what is all this nonsense about not allowing your mother to send for the doctor?'

'Ah, but what can a doctor do? My disease is in my soul. I am stricken by love.' He laughed dryly.

'Will you let me send for him? We can discuss your experiences further when you are in better shape.'

'Very well; if you must. I shall see him. Oh, but what am I to do?'

I got my friend to bed and then sent word to his mother, who on hearing that her son had relented wasted no time in sending for the family physician.

The doctor's opinion was that the patient's condition was one brought on by some great mental excitement, though what the cause of the excitement was he could not discover. Rest and calm were prescribed along with a sleeping draught. It was the following day before Millbrook was once again alert enough to talk and as soon as he was he sent for me. I was relieved to see that he was looking better for his prolonged sleep. He smiled weakly as I entered the room.

'I am sorry to have given you so much trouble yesterday,' said he.

'Not at all,' said I gently. 'I am glad to see you looking more like your old self.'

'I do feel stronger today. But I am still at a loss what to do,' said he despairingly. I did not want to encourage a relapse in his condition so I endeavoured to soothe him as best I could.

'My dear chap, you must not allow yourself to get into such a state. Tell me, calmly, what is your quandary?'

'I am in love; that is my curse and I long more than anything to be with the woman I love. But how can I be? I cannot even be certain that she is real, though I feel in my heart that it is so. But if she is dead already, then how can I join her without suffering my own demise?' I was greatly troubled to hear my friend talking this way. Though I was and am, as my friend had stated, open-minded, I could not help but entertain great concerns for his sanity; yet, something in my own instincts, something subtle and intangible, convinced me that there was more to this than mere delusion. Still, whatever the cause, the risks to my friend's mental and physical safety were real enough. I must do what I could to bring him peace. I thought for a moment. Suddenly, an idea began to suggest itself to me.

'Very well, let us suppose for a moment that what you have experienced is real and is not the result of illness. There is another possibility other than those you have stated.'

'Yes, yes,' he responded eagerly. 'Go on.'

'Well, if you met her whilst suspended between life and death, is it not possible that she likewise was in this condition? That being the case, if her existence is real, then she need not be dead.' My friend seized on this idea with great enthusiasm. But a moment later he fell back on his pillow with a groan, his hand to his brow.

'But even if it were so, how would I ever find her?'

'Well, that is a matter I shall have to give some thought to. You could start by describing her to me.'

'No need. My desk, the draw on the right-hand side.' He motioned to a small desk by the window and I rose and opened the draw indicated. Inside was a delicately rendered pencil drawing of a beautiful young woman. I looked at my friend questioningly.

'I drew it before your arrival yesterday.' He smiled. 'I knew my little hobby would come in useful one day. It is the perfect likeness of her if I say so myself. It was almost as if it drew itself; but then her face is always before me. Oh, I must find her. I don't know what power brought us together, but I must find her again if it takes my last breath.'

'Do not speak that way. We will do all that can be done. For now, you must rest.'

I left him to sleep, taking the picture with me. I sat in my room for some time studying the portrait. She really was remarkably beautiful, with delicate features, high cheekbones, subtly curving full lips, and large round eyes framed with long dark lashes. I could easily understand my friend's infatuation. But how could we ever hope to trace the girl, if, in fact, she lived?

I agreed to stay on for a few days at Millbrook's request. It seemed that the mere hope of finding the girl was enough to revive my friend's flagging spirits, and he was soon looking more like his old self than he had been for some weeks. He had dreamt of the mysterious girl each night and seemed absolutely convinced now that we would find her.

'I feel as though there is a kind of fate at work in the whole thing,' he said to me one morning. The matter still remained, however, of how we were to actually go about finding her.

Over breakfast, I announced my intention of going down to the town to post some letters and to run some small errands. On hearing this Mrs Millbrook said that she was planning on going into town herself after breakfast and if I wished I could ride with her. I thanked her and accepted her offer.

Having arrived in town and made our arrangements to reconvene in an hour's time, we were just on the verge of separating when Mrs Millbrook spotted a neighbour of hers, whom she desired me to meet. She was a tall, handsome, middle-aged woman, who was accompanied by a frail-looking younger woman. The elder of the two was introduced to me as Mrs Marten, who greeted me courteously and said,

'This is my niece, Miss Rosamund Fox. She is staying with me for a few weeks.' The girl acknowledged us graciously, and I, only now looking at her properly for the first time, almost gasped aloud. There before me, quite by chance, on the street was the very girl we had been wondering how to find. I could hardly believe my eyes. This was beyond coincidence; Millbrook was right; there must indeed be a kind of fate involved. I was secretly very glad when Mrs Millbrook invited them to tea the following day and they accepted.

I was in a state of great nervous excitement. I wanted to tell my friend at once, to prepare him, but I thought it prudent not to get his hopes up in case I should be wrong in my identification. I did my best to suppress any outward sign of agitation and bided my time until the two should be brought together. I confess I was fearful; what if he should recognise her but she did not recognise him? What would the effect of such an occurrence be?

All the rest of the day and the following morning I was in a mood of high excitement. I was deeply interested in the outcome of this meeting, not just for my friend's sake but out of an intense curiosity. I have always been fascinated by anything that touched upon the realms of the supernatural or the metaphysical and this was, within my experience, perfectly unique.

At last, the allotted hour came. We were all seated in the drawing room when the guests were shown in. As we rose to greet them I watched with eagerness, first my friend and then Miss Fox. Millbrook staggered as he laid eyes on the girl; a flush of red passed swiftly over his face. His eyes were wide with astonishment. As Miss Fox's eyes came to rest on my friend I was conscious at once of a sudden rigidity in her frame. Her pale face turned paler yet, and she was evidently struggling to contain some strong emotion. In a moment she was in full control of herself once more, and none but Millbrook and I had observed any change in her. Though neither could make any allusion to a prior acquaintanceship before the company, I who knew their secret fancied I could see the recognition and delight in their shy glances and pleasant smiles.

What more is there to tell? The relationship blossomed, and it transpired that Miss Fox had, at about the same time as my friend, also been struck with illness and had lain for some days in a state close to death. As soon as she was enough recovered to travel, her doctor had advised a change of air to complete the cure, and so she had been placed in the care of her aunt, Mrs Marten. She had dreamt of my friend as he had dreamt of her and suffered similarly.

Once a suitable period had passed the two who were already as one in soul became likewise in matrimony, and a happier couple I have never known.

Copyright Information

The stories in this compilation have previously been published elsewhere. The details of the original publications are as follows:

The White Lady © 2014 First published in A Spirited Evening and Other Stories.

Three Knocks © 2014 First published in A Spirited Evening and Other Stories.

A Spirited Evening © 2014 First published in A Spirited Evening and Other Stories.

The Darkness Within © 2014 First published in A Spirited Evening and Other Stories.

A Most Unusual Disturbance © 2014 First published in A Spirited Evening and Other Stories.

Made in the USA
Middletown, DE
28 September 2019